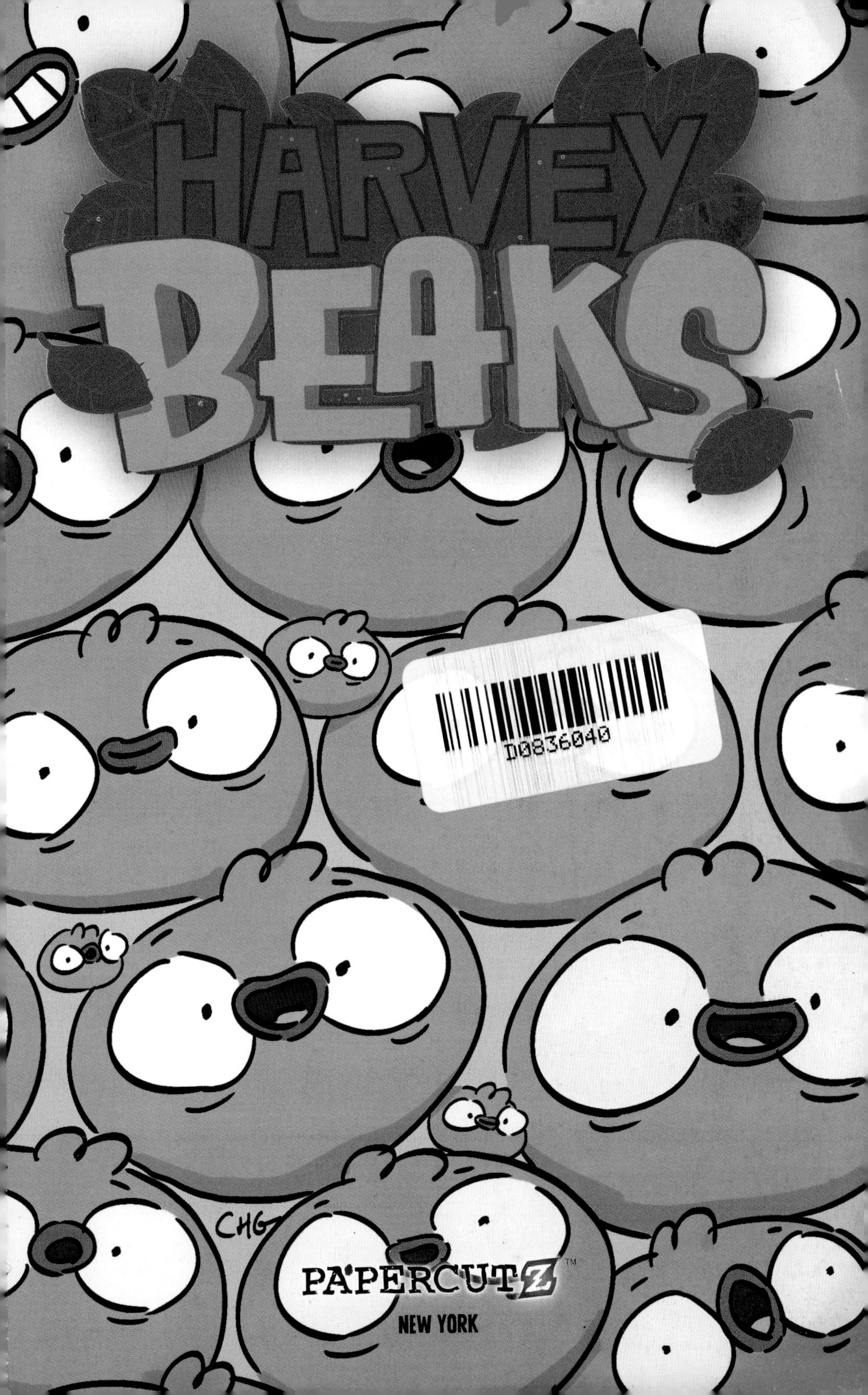
HARVEY BEAKS
CHG
PAPERCUTZ™
NEW YORK

NICKELODEON GRAPHIC NOVELS AVAILABLE FROM PAPERCUTZ

#1 "Fight the Future with Flavor"

#2 "New Kid on the Block"

#3 "Story Time with Sanjay and Craig"

#1 "Journey to the Bottom of the Seats"

#2 "Buhdeuce Rocks the Rocket"

#1 "Inside Joke"

#2 "It's Crazy Time"

COMING SOON!

#1 Nickelodeon Pandemonium

COMING SOON!

#1 "Orgle Borgle Selfie Simple-Dee-Doo!"

Nickelodeon graphic novels are available for $7.99 in paperback, $12.99 in hardcover. Available from booksellers everywhere. You can also order online from Papercutz.com, or call 1-800-886-1223, Monday through Friday, 9-5 EST. MC, Visa, and AmEx accepted. To order by mail, please add $4.00 for postage and handling for first book ordered, $1.00 for each additional book and make check payable to NBM Publishing. Send to: Papercutz, 160 Broadway, Suite 700, East Wing, New York, NY 10038.

Nickelodeon graphic novels are also available digitally wherever e-books are sold.

SUBSCRIBE!

Never miss an issue of nickelodeon™ MAGAZINE

Get Your Copies Delivered Right to Your Mailbox at Home!

ORDER ONLINE at Papercutz.com/nickmag

OR CALL 1-800-778-6278

(Please have debit/credit card ready)

Use promo code: HBGN2.

Save! And Get Free Issues!

7 ISSUES FOR THE PRICE OF 6!

+SAVE $7 OFF COVER PRICE!

6 REGULAR ISSUES
+1 BONUS FREE ISSUE
7 ISSUES FOR ONLY $27.50

14 ISSUES FOR THE PRICE OF 12!

+SAVE $14 OFF COVER PRICE!

12 REGULAR ISSUES
+2 BONUS FREE ISSUES
14 ISSUES FOR ONLY $49.99

DIGITAL SUBSCRIPTION - ONLY $19.99 - OR FREE FOR ALL PRINT SUBSCRIBERS!

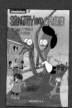

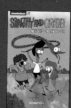

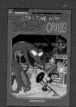

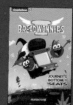

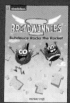

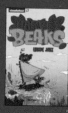

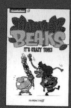

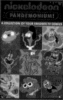

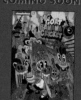

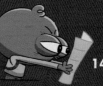

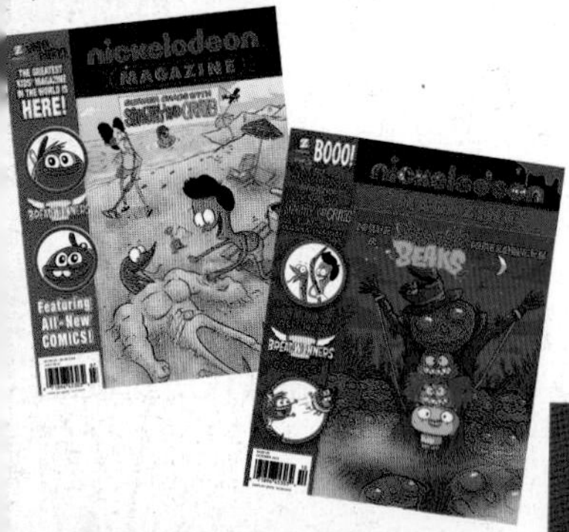

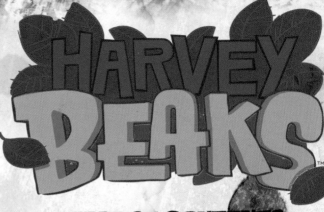

HARVEY BEAKS™

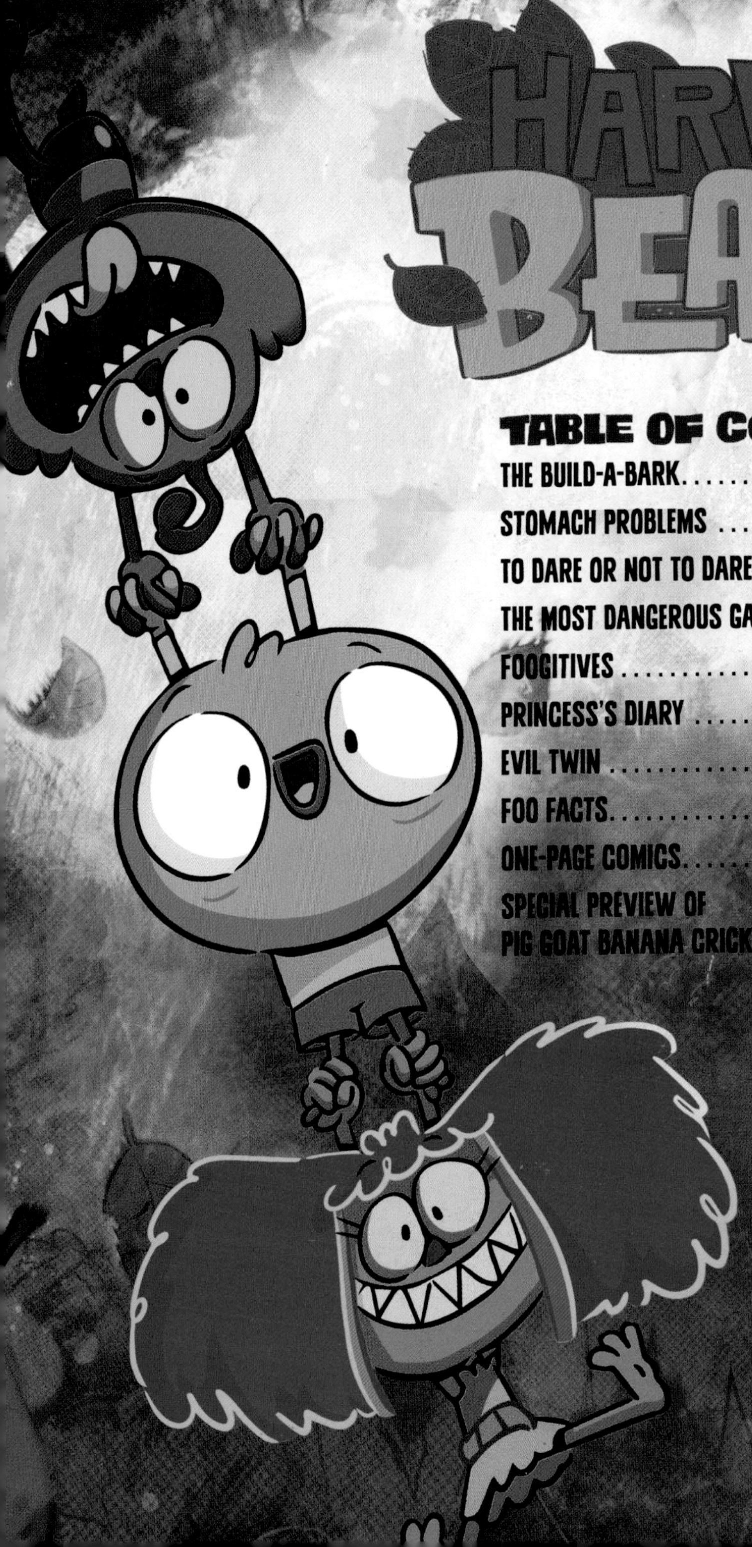

TABLE OF CONTENTS

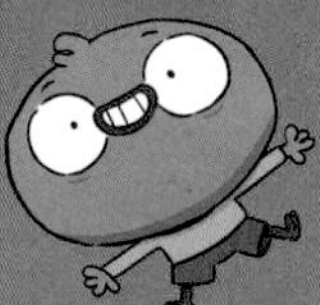

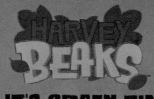

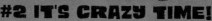

HARVEY BEAKS

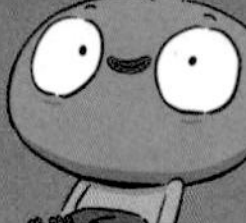

#2 IT'S CRAZY TIME!

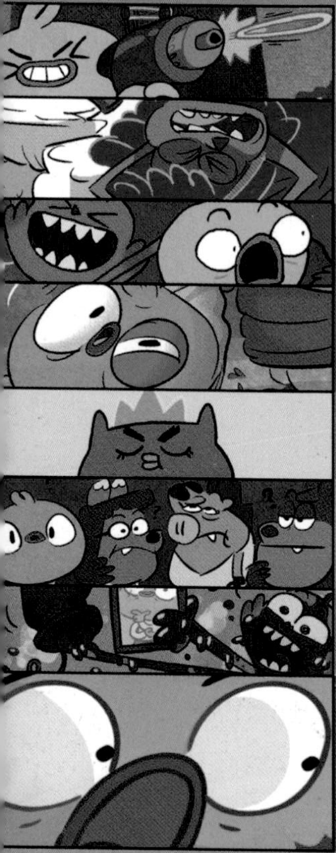

"THE BUILD-A-BARK"
KEVIN KRAMER - WRITER
BRANDON B - ARTIST, LETTERER, AND COLORIST

"STOMACH PROBLEMS"
CARSON MONTGOMERY - WRITER
ANDREAS SCHUSTER - ARTIST & LETTERER
MATT HERMS - COLORIST

"TO DARE OR NOT TO DARE"
KEVIN KRAMER - WRITER
BRANDON B- ARTIST, LETTERER, AND COLORIST

"FOOGITIVES"
SHANE HOUGHTON - WRITER
ANDREAS SCHUSTER - ARTIST & LETTERER
LAURIE E. SMITH - COLORIST

"PRINCESS'S DIARY"
CARSON MONTGOMERY - WRITER
BRANDON B - ARTIST, LETTERER, AND COLORIST

"EVIL TWIN"
SHANE HOUGHTON - WRITER
ANDREAS SCHUSTER - ARTIST & LETTERER
MATTEO BALDRIGHI - COLORIST

"FOO FACTS"
CARSON MONTGOMERY - WRITER
BRANDON B - ARTIST, LETTERER, AND COLORIST

PGS. 15, 24, 32, 44, 52, 62: ONE-PAGE COMICS
15 DAVID TEAS - WRITER AND ARTIST
24 CHARLIE GAVIN - WRITER AND ARTIST
32 CELESTINO MARINA - WRITER AND ARTIST
44 AMALIA LEVARI AND NIKI LOPEZ- WRITERS, NIKI LOPEZ - ARTIST
52 ANNA O'BRIAN - WRITER AND ARTIST
62 SAEID ZAMENIATENI - WRITER AND ARTIST

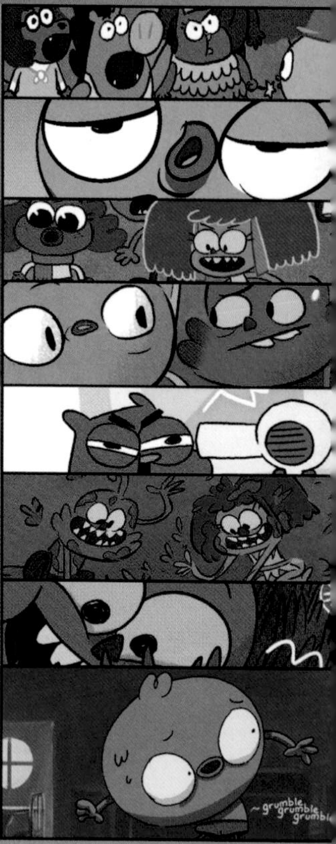
~grumble grumble grumble

BASED ON THE NICKELODEON ANIMATED TV SERIES CREATED BY C.H. GREENBLATT

COVER - ANDREAS SCHUSTER, ARTIST AND COLORIST

JAMES SALERNO - SR. ART DIRECTOR/NICKELODEON
CHRIS NELSON - DESIGN/PRODUCTION
JEFF WHITMAN - PRODUCTION COORDINATOR
BETHANY BRYAN - EDITOR
JOAN HILTY - COMICS EDITOR/NICKELODEON
ISABELLA VAN INGEN - EDITORIAL INTERN
JIM SALICRUP
EDITOR-IN-CHIEF

ISBN: 978-1-62991-468-8 PAPERBACK EDITION
ISBN: 978-1-62991-469-5 HARDCOVER EDITION

PAPERCUTZ BOOKS MAY BE PURCHASED FOR BUSINESS OR PROMOTIONAL USE. FOR INFORMATION ON BULK PURCHASES PLEASE CONTACT MACMILLAN CORPORATE AND PREMIUM SALES DEPARTMENT AT (800) 221-7945 X5442.

PRINTED IN CHINA JUNE 2016 BY IMAGO
SHENZHEN MEIDA PRINTING CO., LTD.
NO. 347, PING LONG EAST RD., PING HU,
LONGJIANG DISTRICT, SHENZHEN 518111
CHINA

DISTRIBUTED BY MACMILLAN
FIRST PRINTING

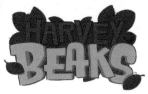

THE BUILD-A-BARK

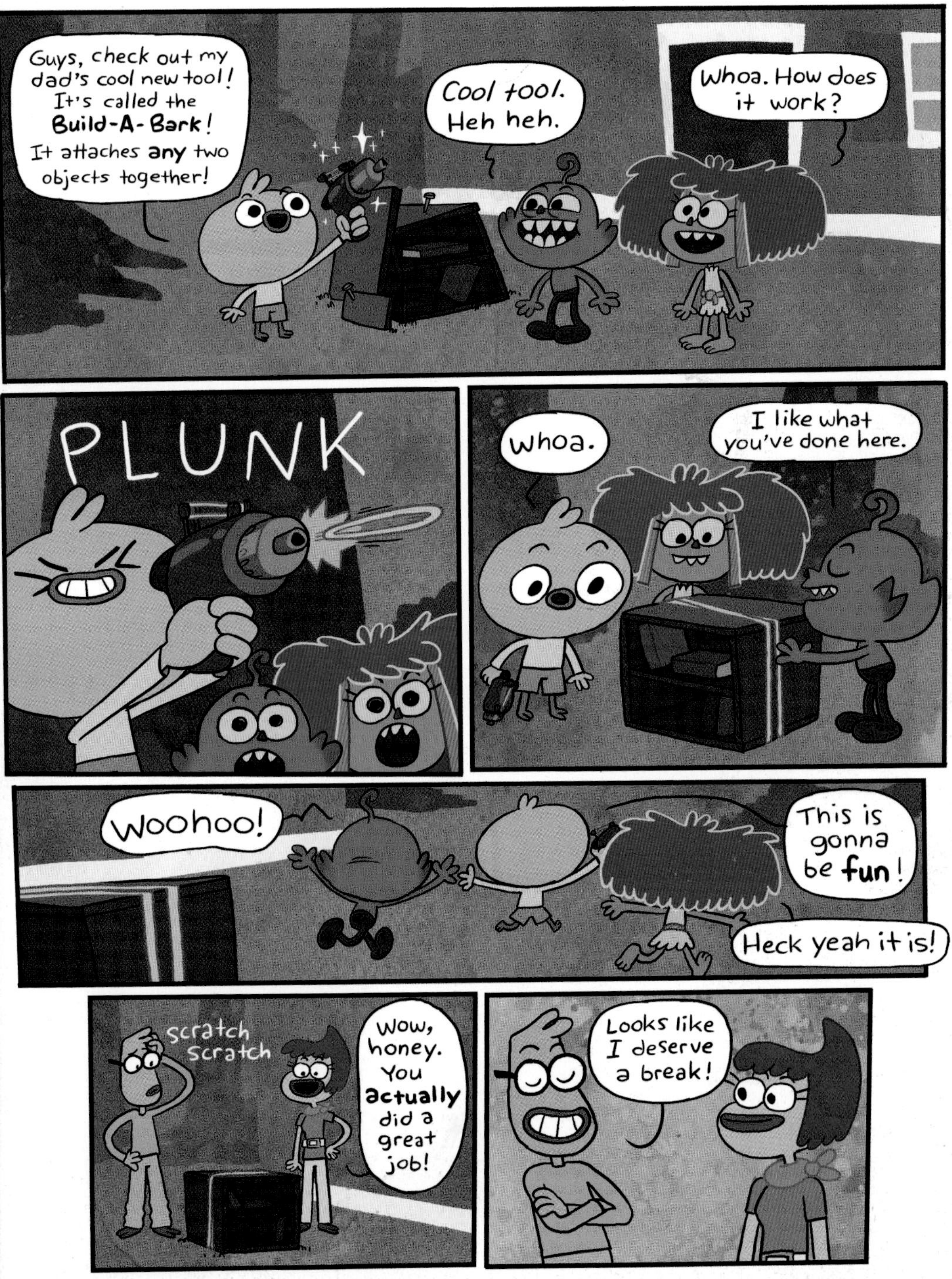

Guys, check out my dad's cool new tool! It's called the **Build-A-Bark**! It attaches **any** two objects together!
Cool tool. Heh heh.
Whoa. How does it work?
PLUNK
Whoa.
I like what you've done here.
Woohoo!
This is gonna be **fun**!
Heck yeah it is!
scratch scratch
Wow, honey. You **actually** did a great job!
Looks like I deserve a break!

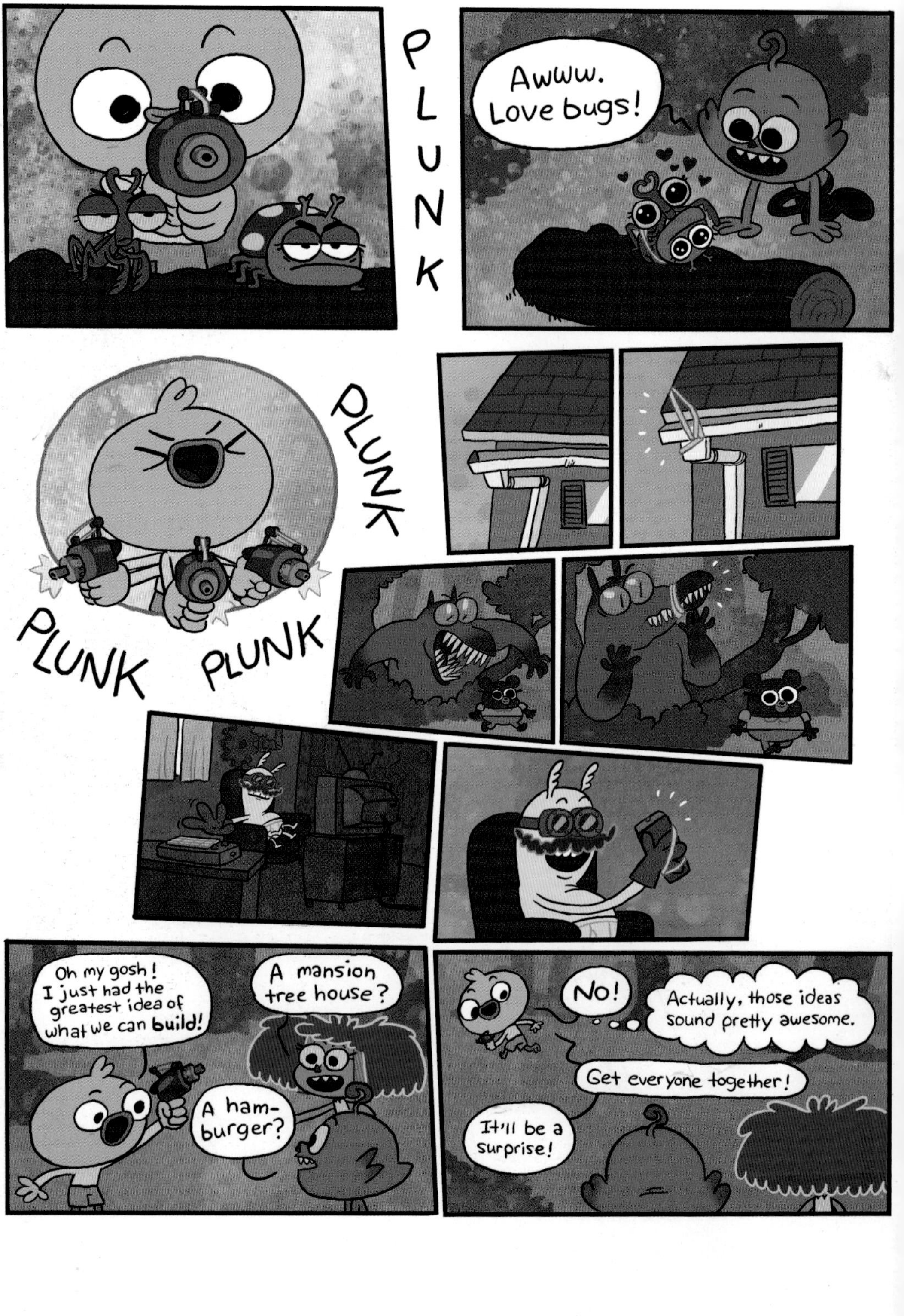
PLUNK
Awww. Love bugs!
PLUNK
PLUNK
PLUNK
Oh my gosh! I just had the greatest idea of what we can **build**!
A mansion tree house?
A ham-burger?
No!
Actually, those ideas sound pretty awesome.
Get everyone together!
It'll be a surprise!

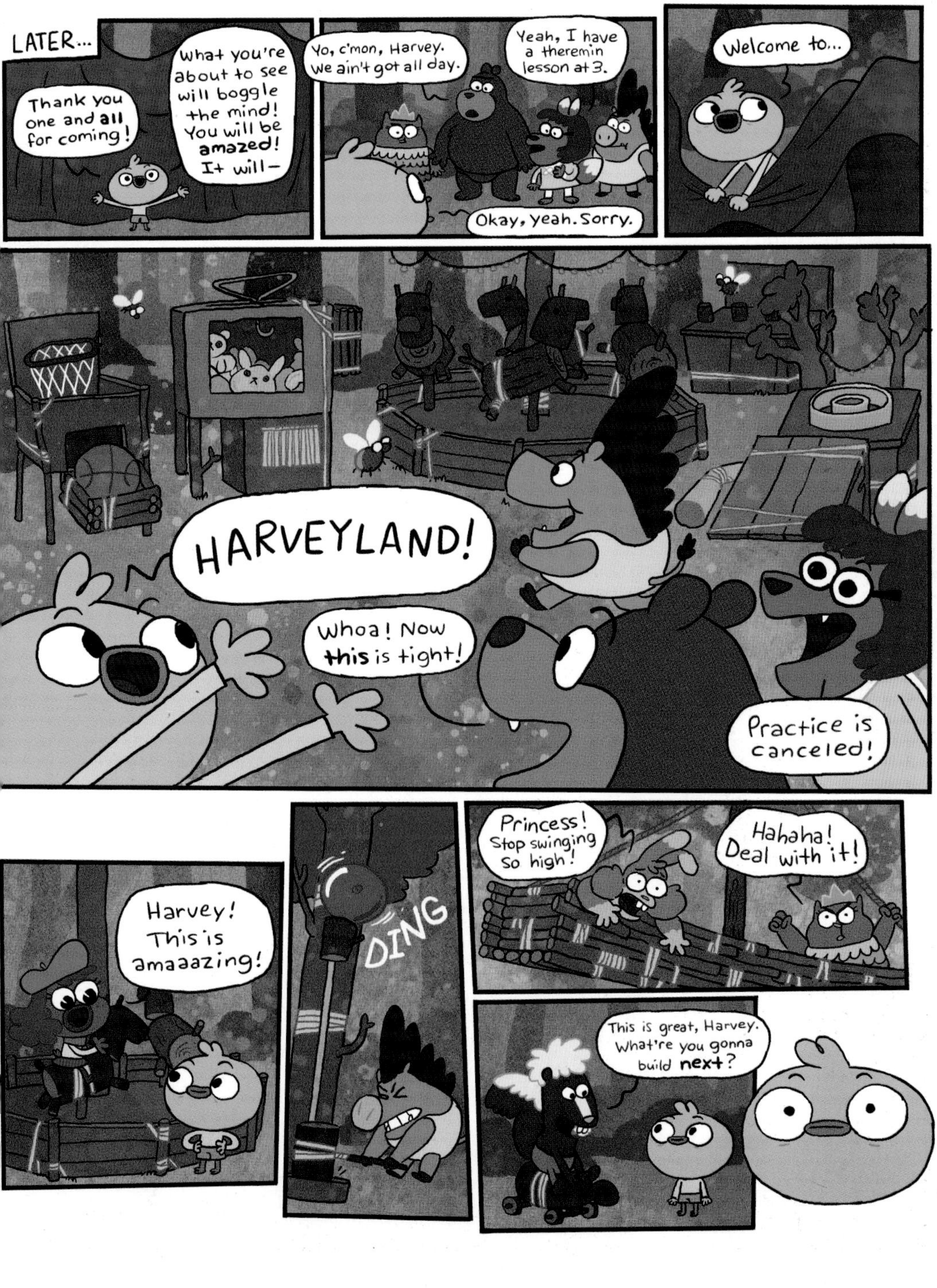

LATER...
Thank you one and **all** for coming!
What you're about to see will boggle the mind! You will be **amazed**! It will—
Yo, c'mon, Harvey. We ain't got all day.
Yeah, I have a theremin lesson at 3.
Okay, yeah. Sorry.
Welcome to...
HARVEYLAND!
Whoa! Now **this** is tight!
Practice is canceled!
Harvey! This is amaaazing!
DING
Princess! Stop swinging so high!
Hahaha! Deal with it!
This is great, Harvey. What're you gonna build **next**?

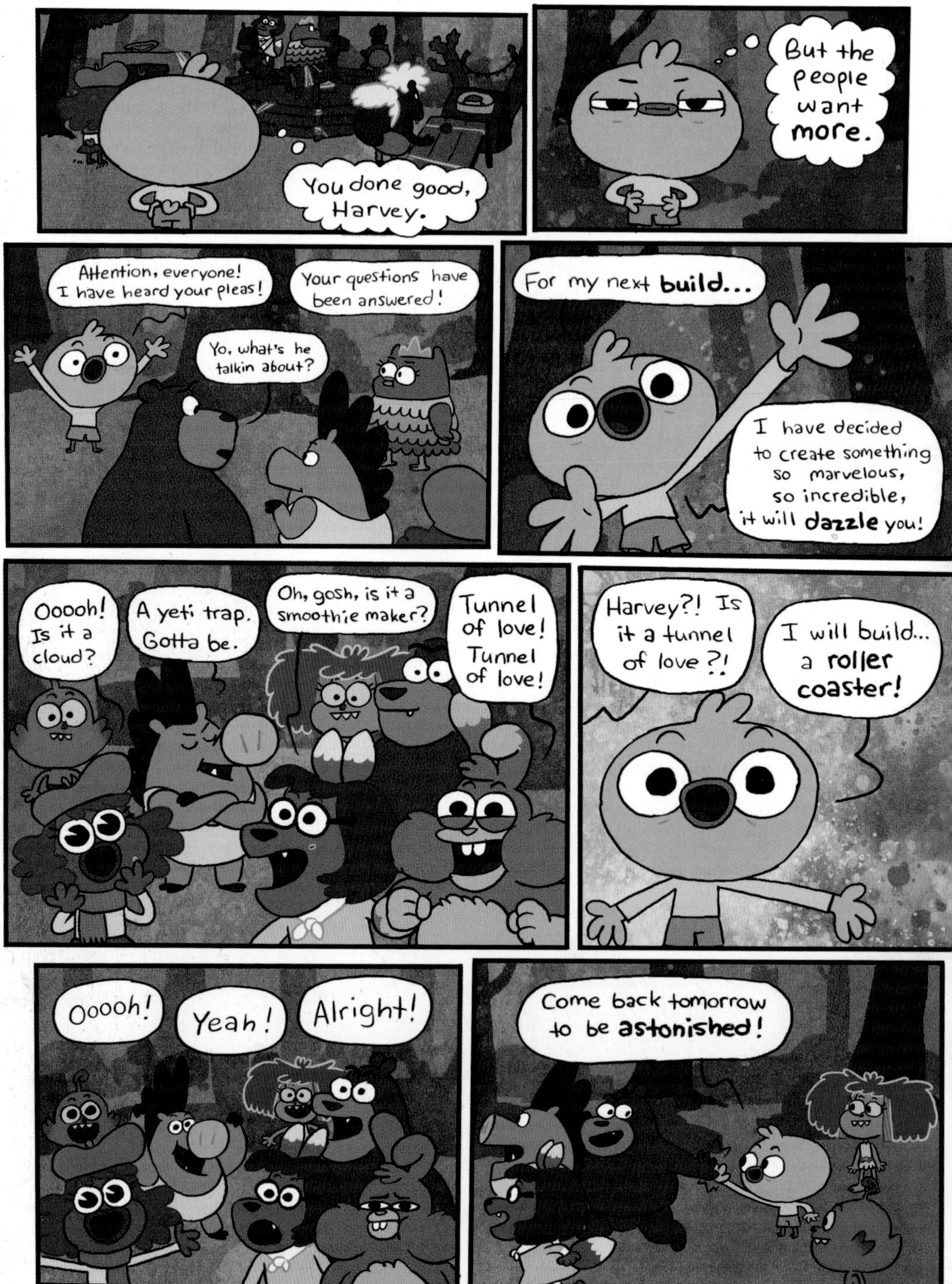
You done good, Harvey.
But the people want more.
Attention, everyone! I have heard your pleas!
Your questions have been answered!
Yo, what's he talkin about?
For my next **build...**
I have decided to create something so marvelous, so incredible, it will **dazzle** you!
Ooooh! Is it a cloud?
A yeti trap. Gotta be.
Oh, gosh, is it a smoothie maker?
Tunnel of love! Tunnel of love!
Harvey?! Is it a tunnel of love?!
I will build... a **roller coaster!**
Ooooh!
Yeah!
Alright!
Come back tomorrow to be **astonished!**

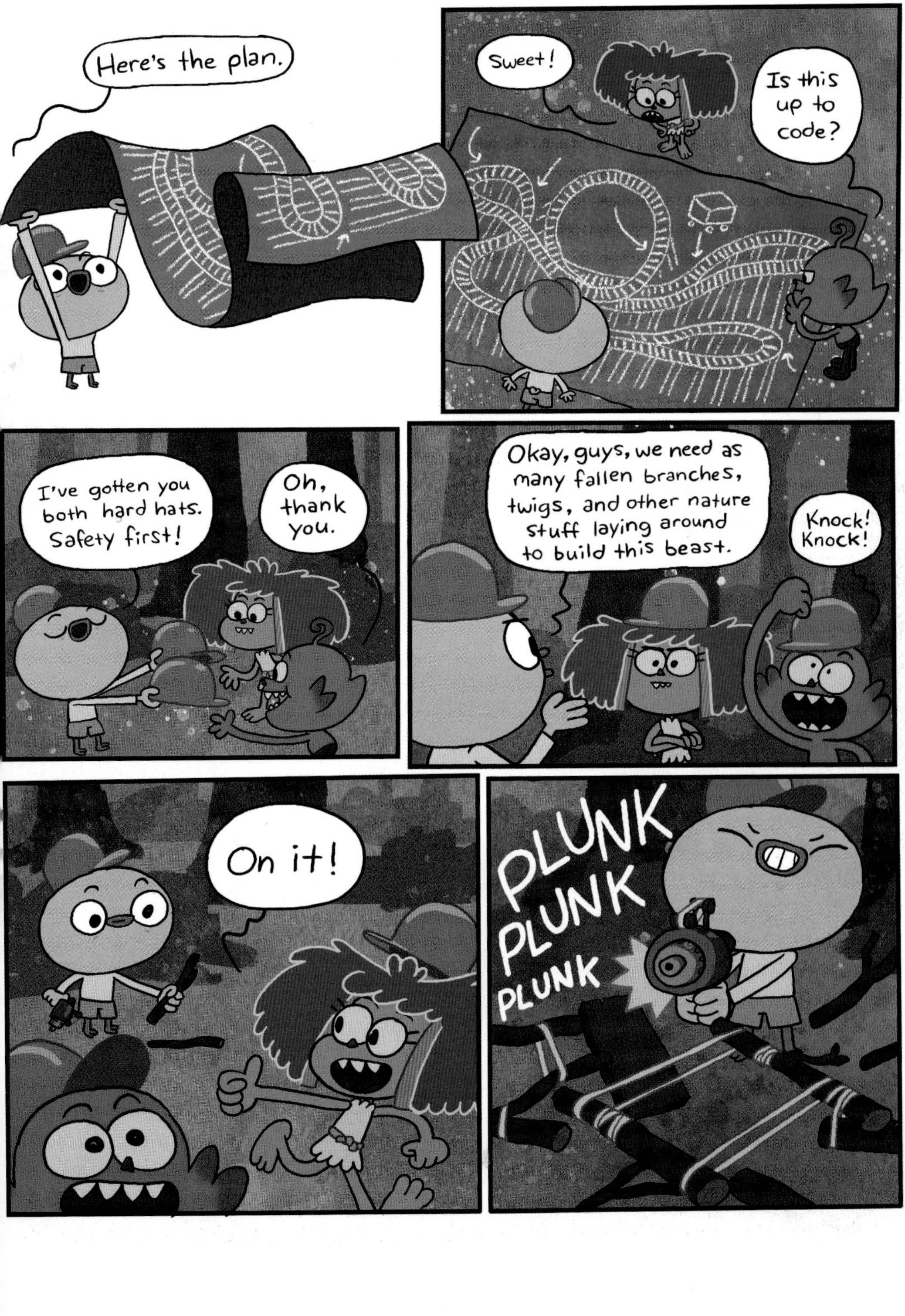
Here's the plan.
Sweet!
Is this up to code?
I've gotten you both hard hats. Safety first!
Oh, thank you.
Okay, guys, we need as many fallen branches, twigs, and other nature stuff laying around to build this beast.
Knock! Knock!
On it!
PLUNK
PLUNK
PLUNK
PLUNK

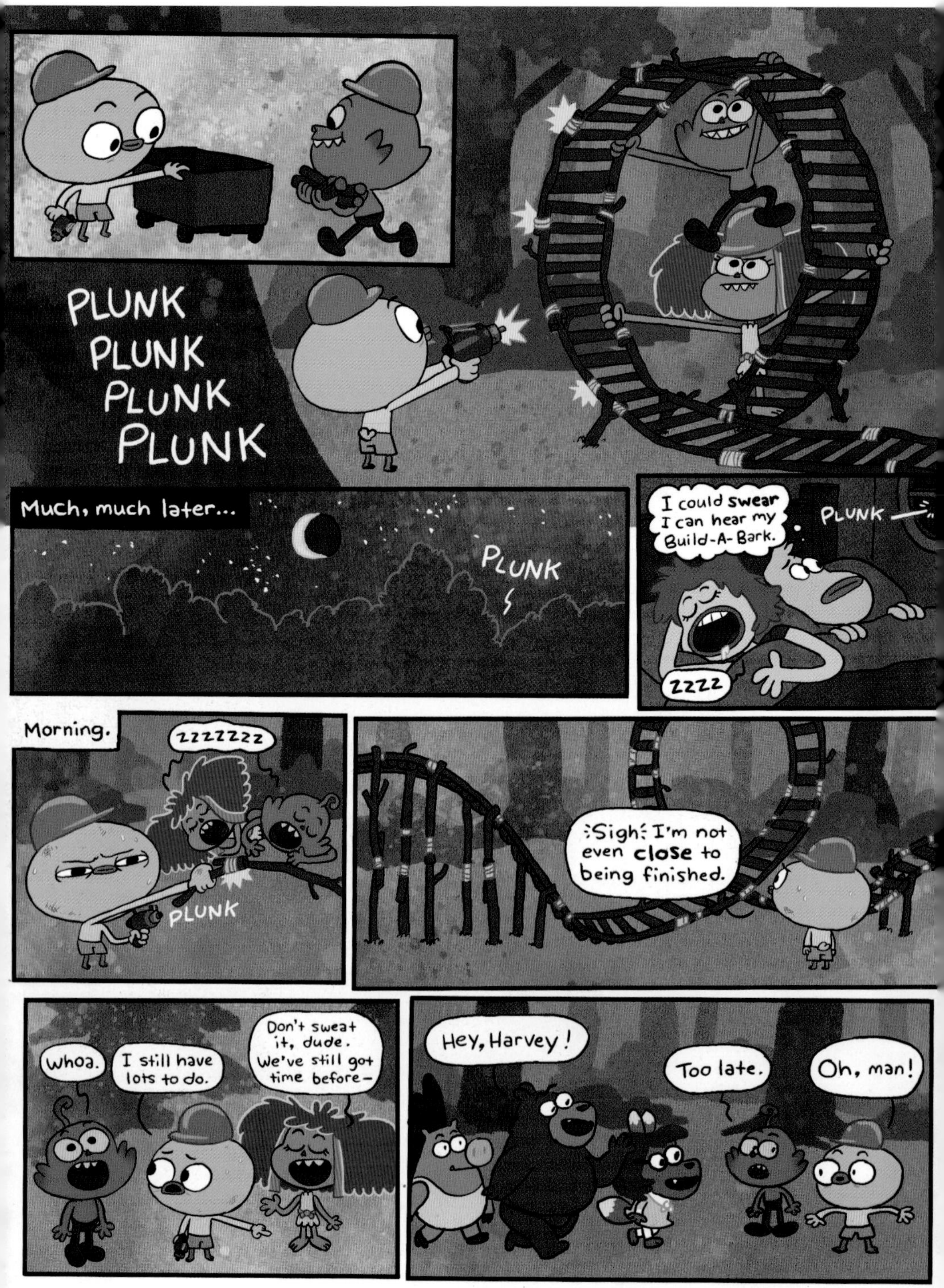
PLUNK
PLUNK
PLUNK
PLUNK
Much, much later...
PLUNK
I could swear I can hear my Build-A-Bark.
PLUNK
ZZZZ
Morning.
ZZZZZZZ
PLUNK
:Sigh: I'm not even close to being finished.
Whoa.
I still have lots to do.
Don't sweat it, dude. We've still got time before—
Hey, Harvey!
Too late.
Oh, man!

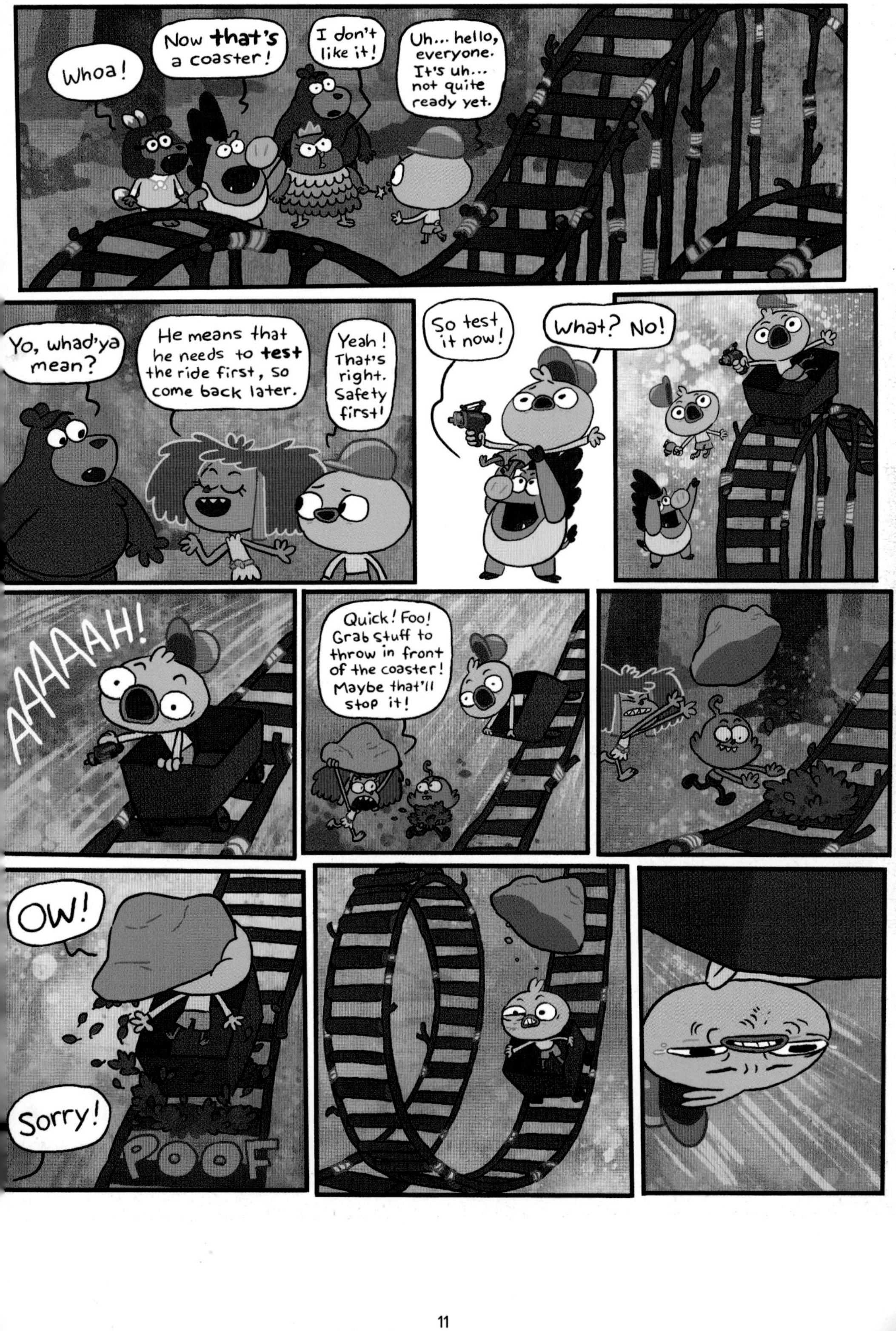
Whoa!
Now that's a coaster!
I don't like it!
Uh... hello, everyone. It's uh... not quite ready yet.
Yo, whad'ya mean?
He means that he needs to test the ride first, so come back later.
Yeah! That's right. Safety first!
So test it now!
What? No!
AAAAAH!
Quick! Foo! Grab stuff to throw in front of the coaster! Maybe that'll stop it!
OW!
Sorry!
POOF

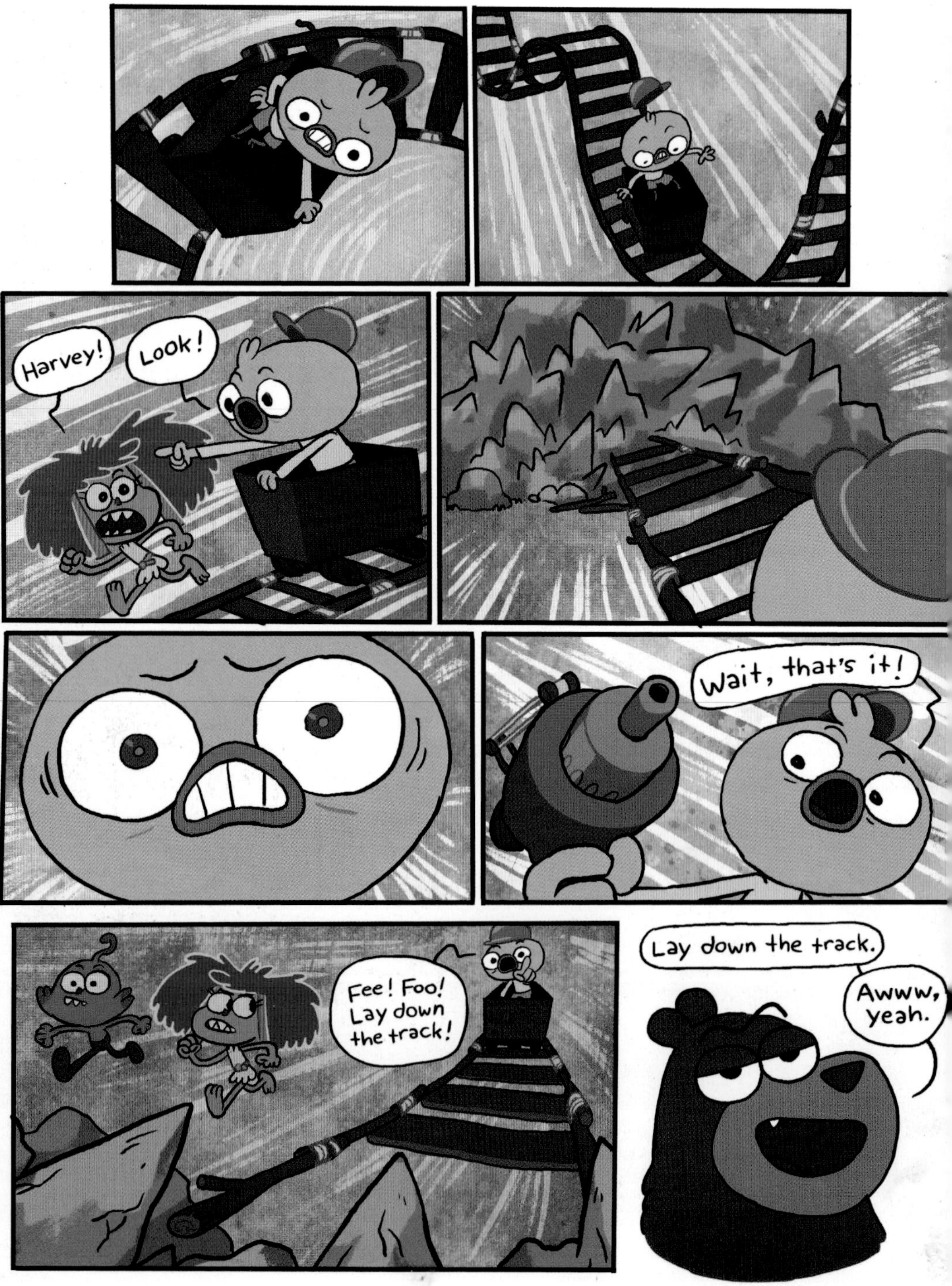

Harvey!
Look!
Wait, that's it!
Fee! Foo! Lay down the track!
Lay down the track.
Awww, yeah.

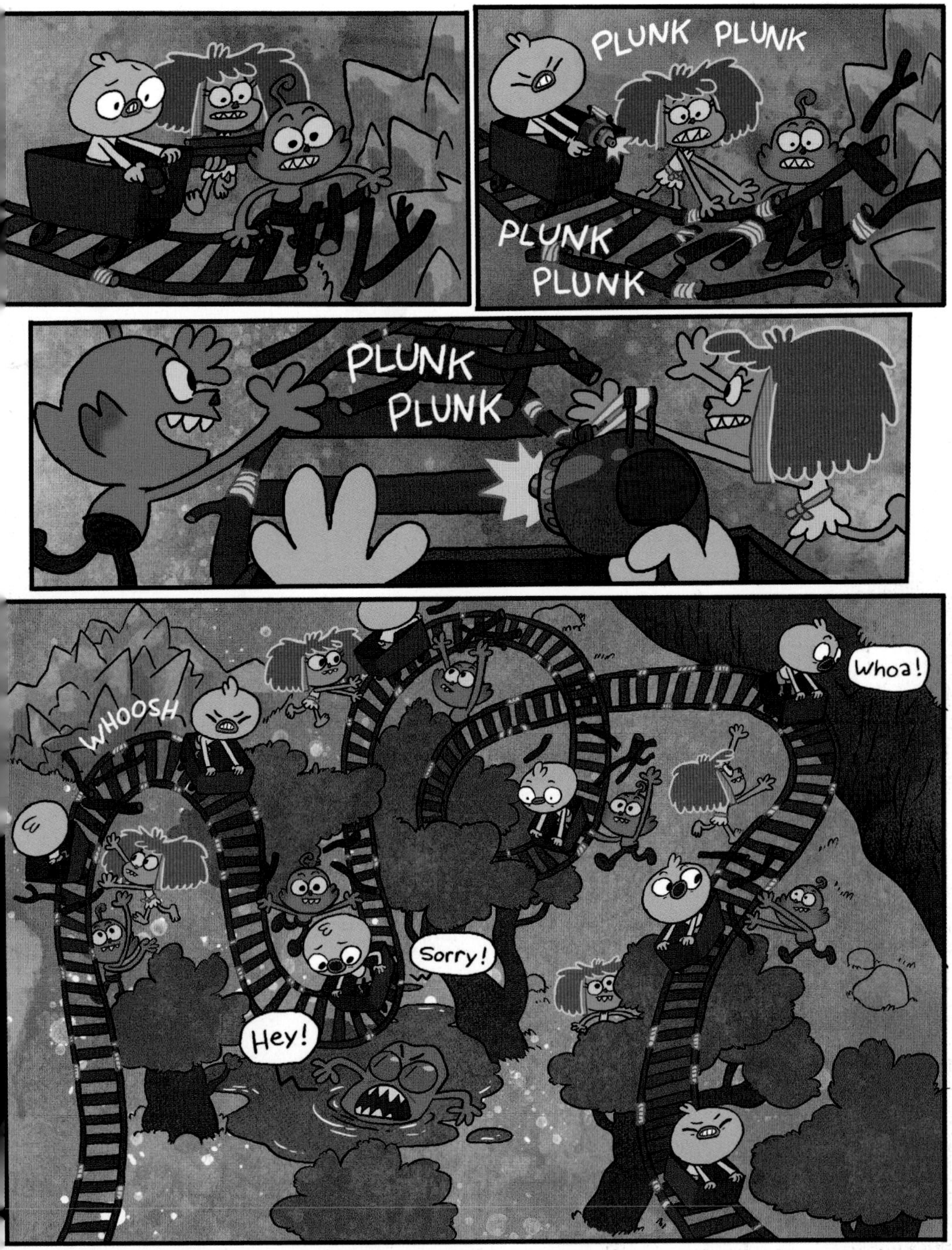
PLUNK PLUNK
PLUNK
PLUNK
PLUNK
PLUNK
WHOOSH
Whoa!
Sorry!
Hey!

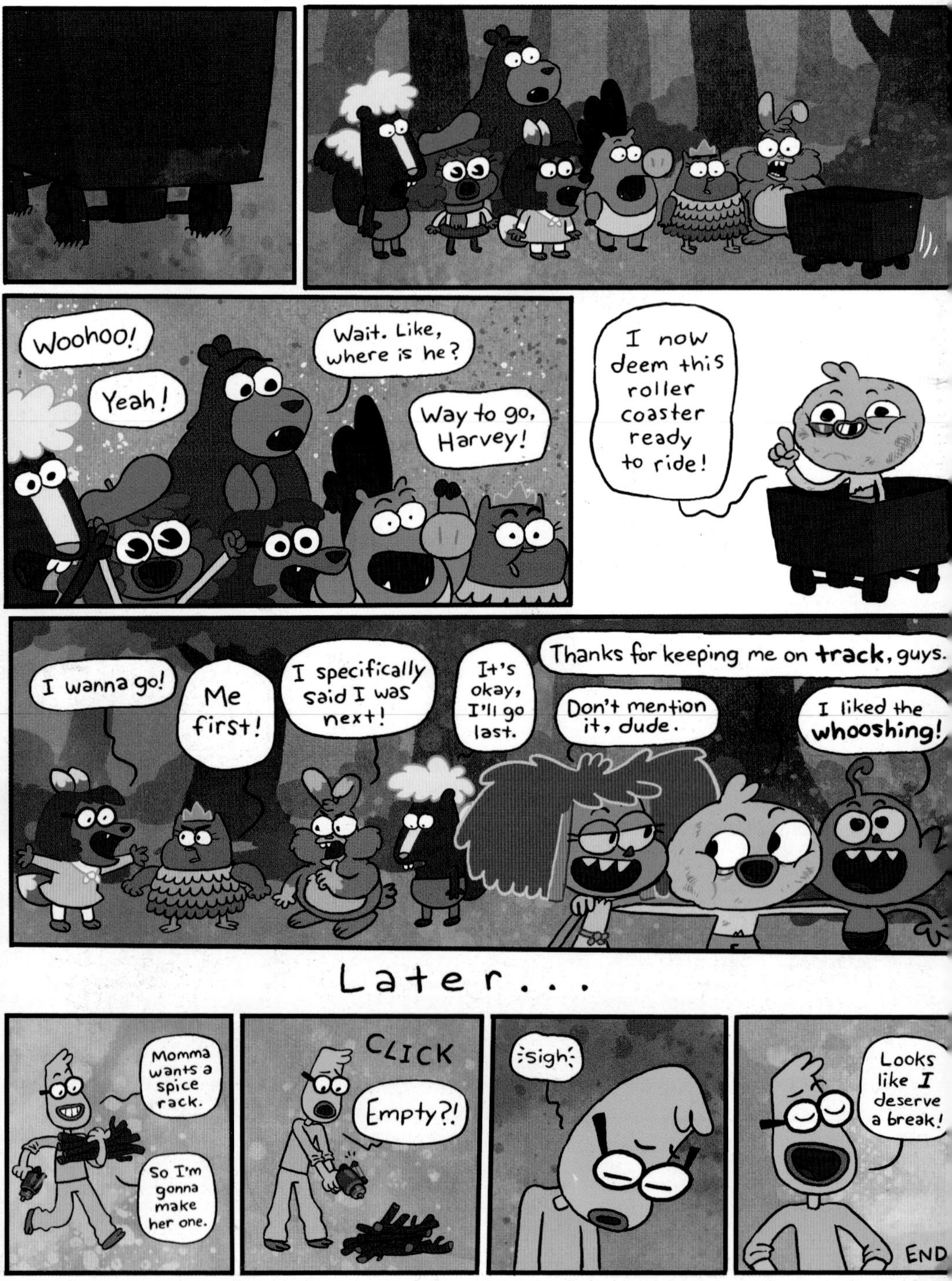
Woohoo!
Yeah!
Wait. Like, where is he?
Way to go, Harvey!
I now deem this roller coaster ready to ride!
I wanna go!
Me first!
I specifically said I was next!
It's okay, I'll go last.
Thanks for keeping me on **track**, guys.
Don't mention it, dude.
I liked the **whooshing**!
Later...
Momma wants a spice rack.
So I'm gonna make her one.
CLICK
Empty?!
:sigh:
Looks like *I* deserve a break!
END

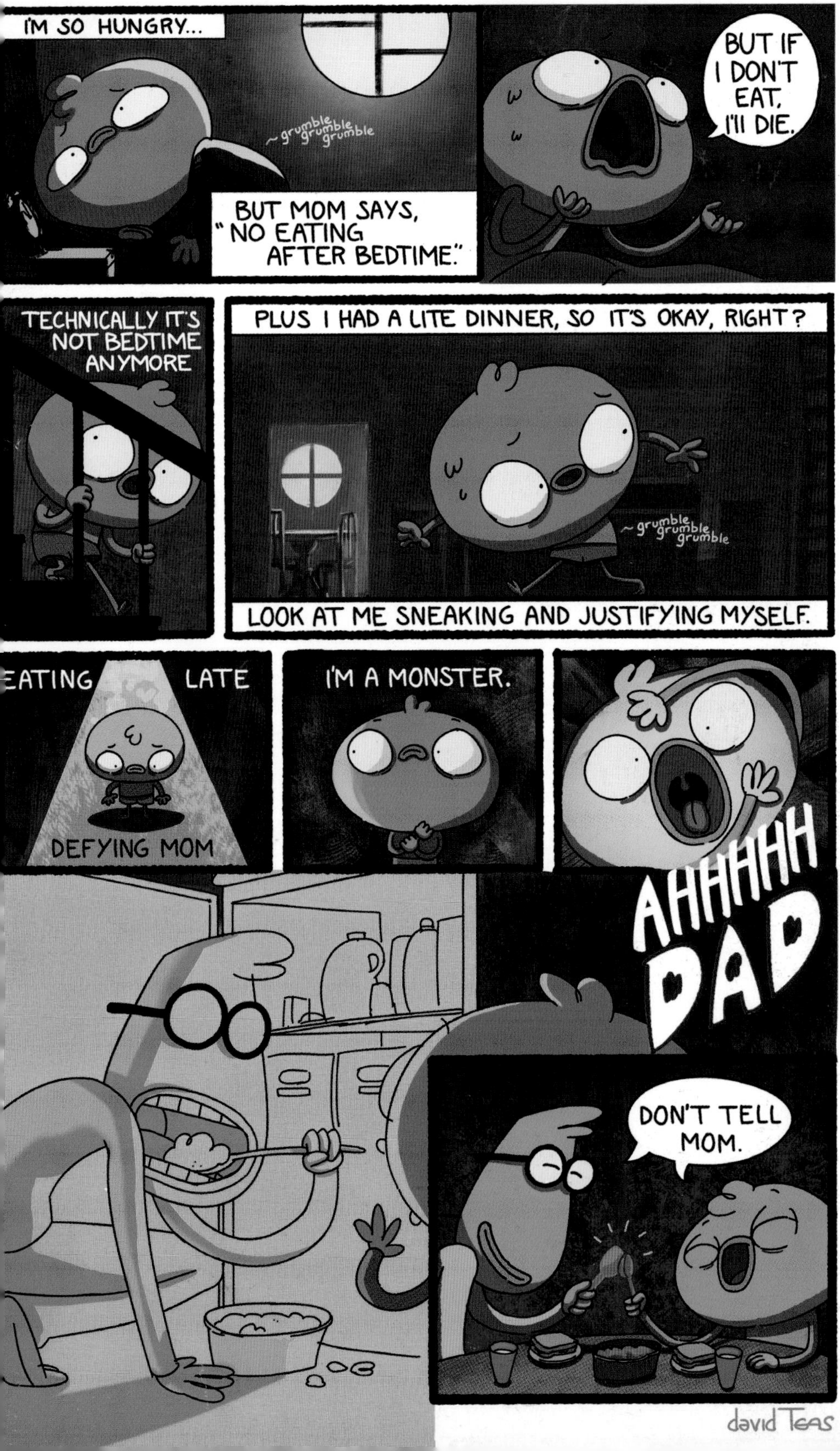
I'M SO HUNGRY...
~grumble grumble grumble
BUT MOM SAYS, "NO EATING AFTER BEDTIME."
BUT IF I DON'T EAT, I'LL DIE.
TECHNICALLY IT'S NOT BEDTIME ANYMORE
PLUS I HAD A LITE DINNER, SO IT'S OKAY, RIGHT?
~grumble grumble grumble
LOOK AT ME SNEAKING AND JUSTIFYING MYSELF.
EATING
LATE
DEFYING MOM
I'M A MONSTER.
AHHHHH
DAD
DON'T TELL MOM.
david Teas

FOO FACT # 8 - GRASS

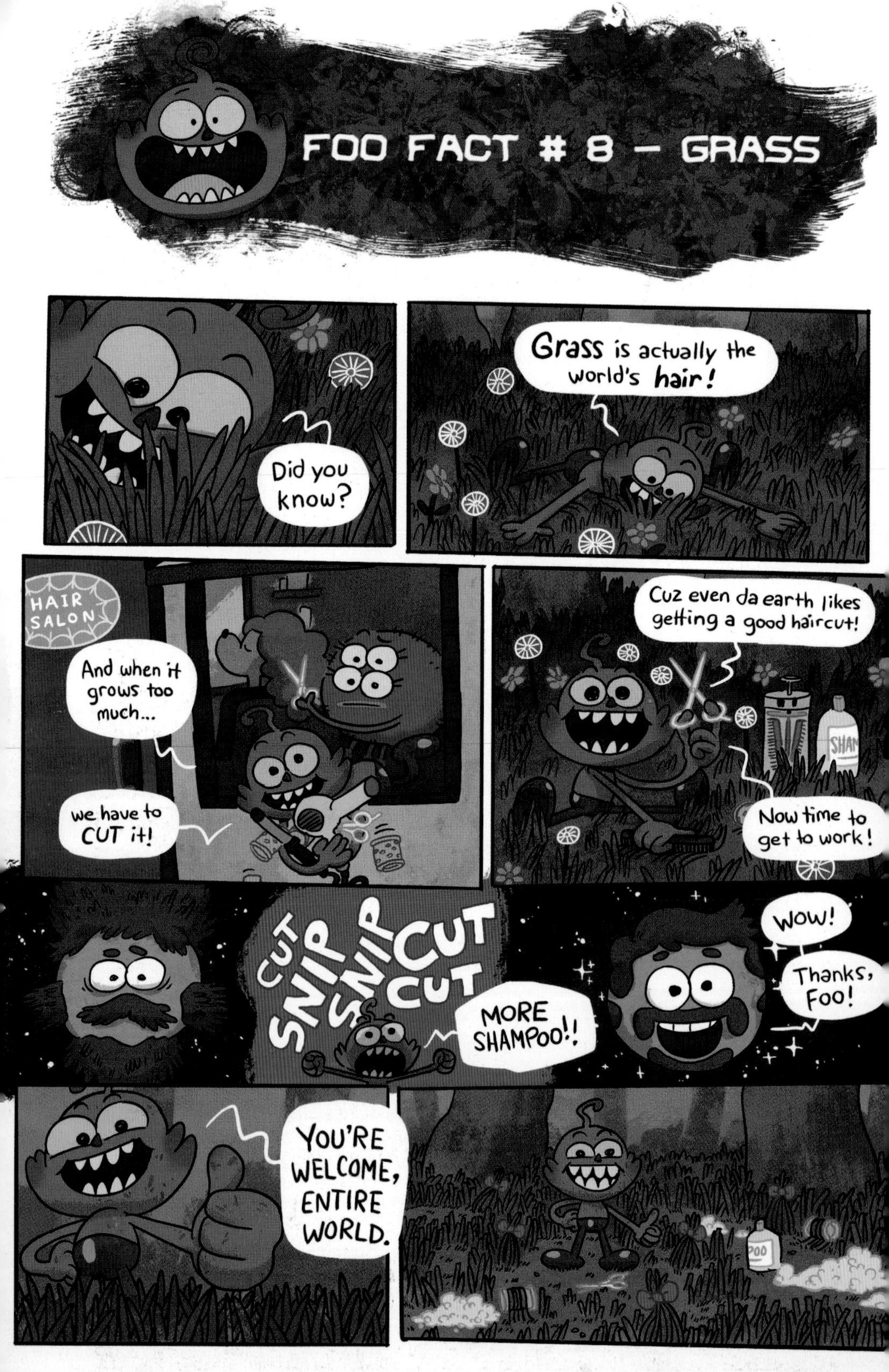
Did you know?
Grass is actually the world's hair!
HAIR SALON
And when it grows too much...
we have to CUT it!
Cuz even da earth likes getting a good haircut!
SHAM
Now time to get to work!
CUT SNIP SNIP CUT
CUT
MORE SHAMPOO!!
WOW!
Thanks, Foo!
YOU'RE WELCOME, ENTIRE WORLD.
POO

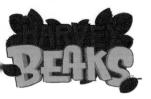

STOMACH PROBLEMS

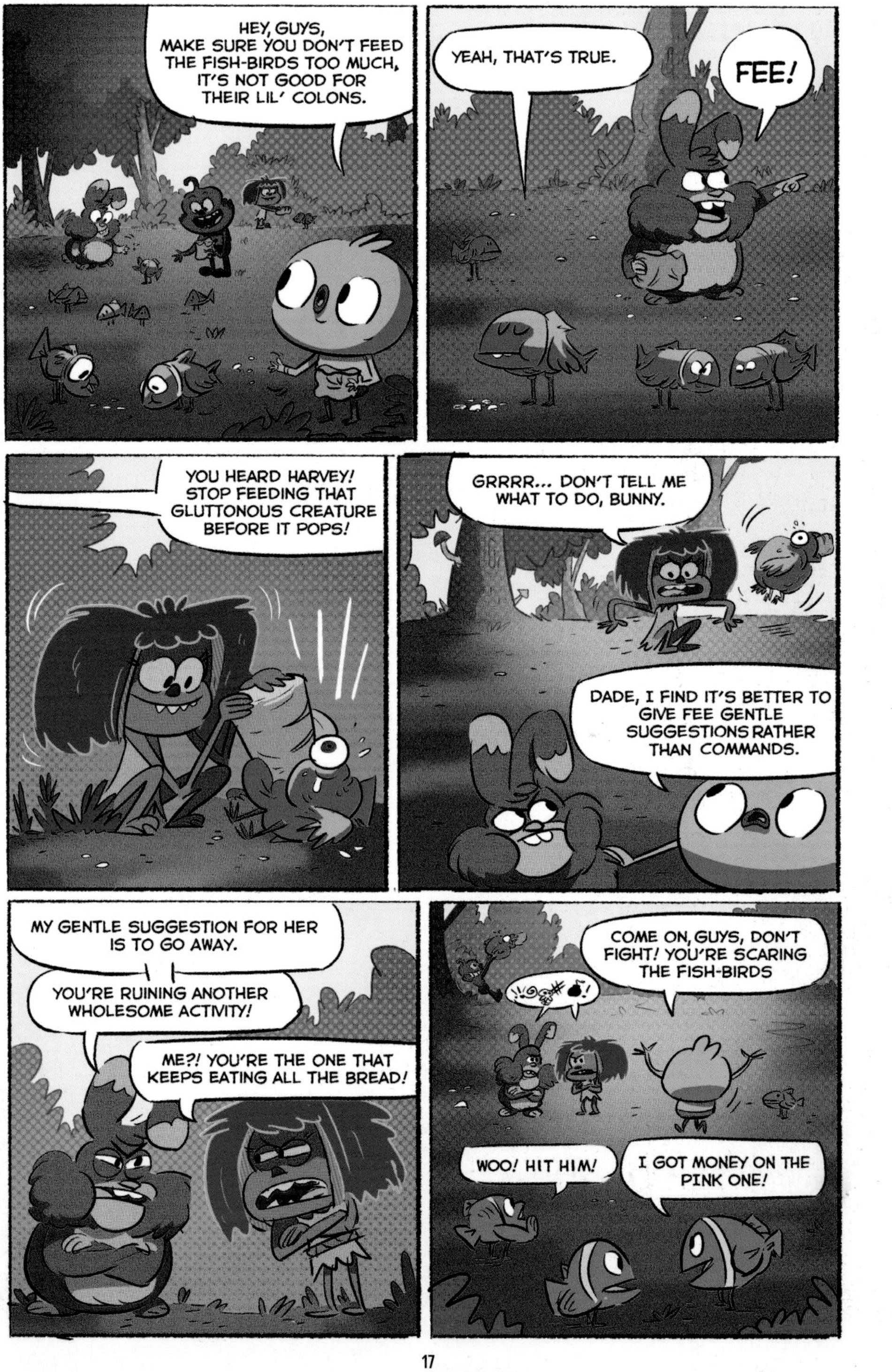

HEY, GUYS, MAKE SURE YOU DON'T FEED THE FISH-BIRDS TOO MUCH, IT'S NOT GOOD FOR THEIR LIL' COLONS.
YEAH, THAT'S TRUE.
FEE!
YOU HEARD HARVEY! STOP FEEDING THAT GLUTTONOUS CREATURE BEFORE IT POPS!
GRRRR... DON'T TELL ME WHAT TO DO, BUNNY.
DADE, I FIND IT'S BETTER TO GIVE FEE GENTLE SUGGESTIONS RATHER THAN COMMANDS.
MY GENTLE SUGGESTION FOR HER IS TO GO AWAY.
YOU'RE RUINING ANOTHER WHOLESOME ACTIVITY!
ME?! YOU'RE THE ONE THAT KEEPS EATING ALL THE BREAD!
COME ON, GUYS, DON'T FIGHT! YOU'RE SCARING THE FISH-BIRDS
WOO! HIT HIM!
I GOT MONEY ON THE PINK ONE!

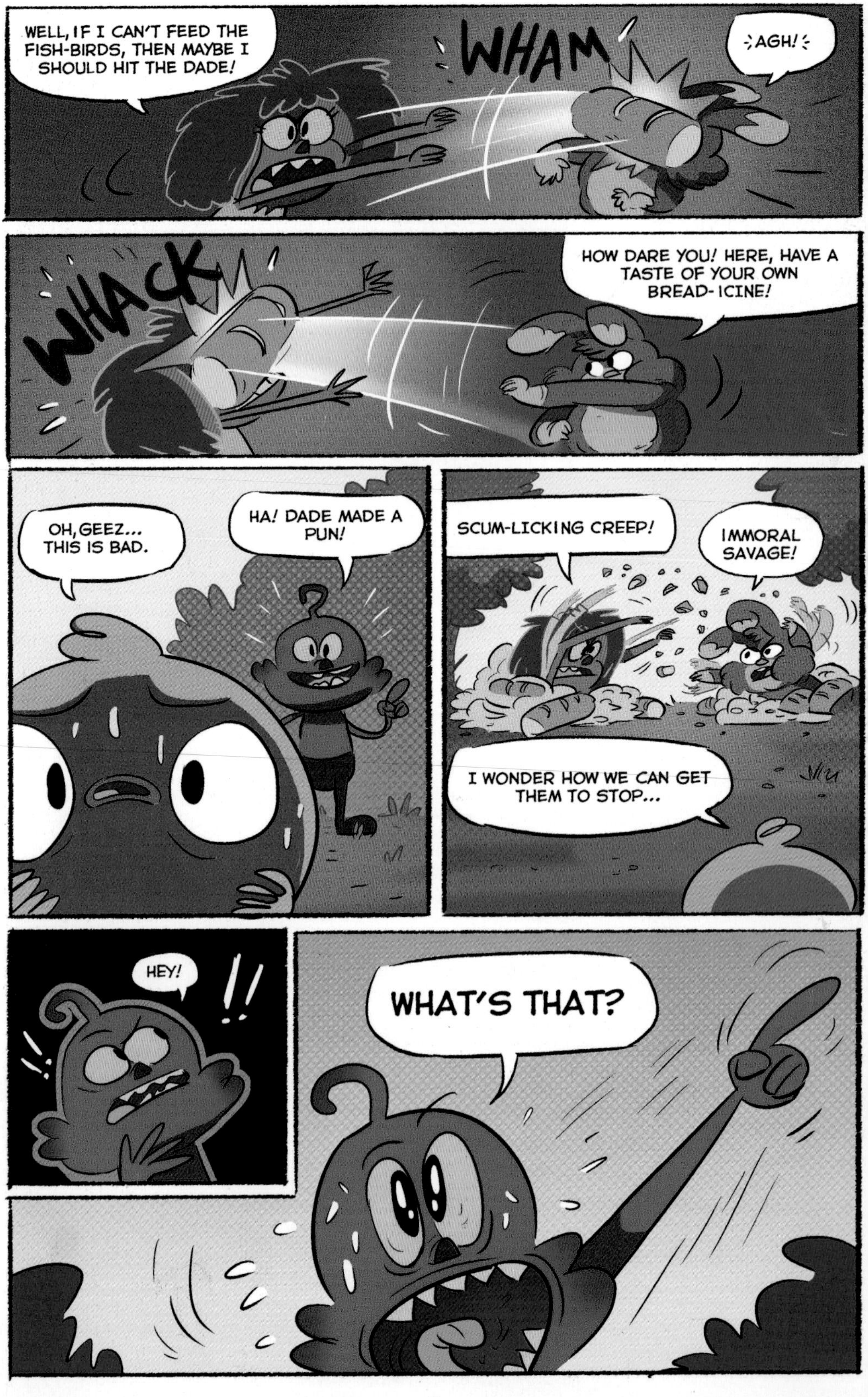
WELL, IF I CAN'T FEED THE FISH-BIRDS, THEN MAYBE I SHOULD HIT THE DADE!
WHAM
AGH!
WHACK
HOW DARE YOU! HERE, HAVE A TASTE OF YOUR OWN BREAD-ICINE!
OH, GEEZ... THIS IS BAD.
HA! DADE MADE A PUN!
SCUM-LICKING CREEP!
IMMORAL SAVAGE!
I WONDER HOW WE CAN GET THEM TO STOP...
HEY!
WHAT'S THAT?

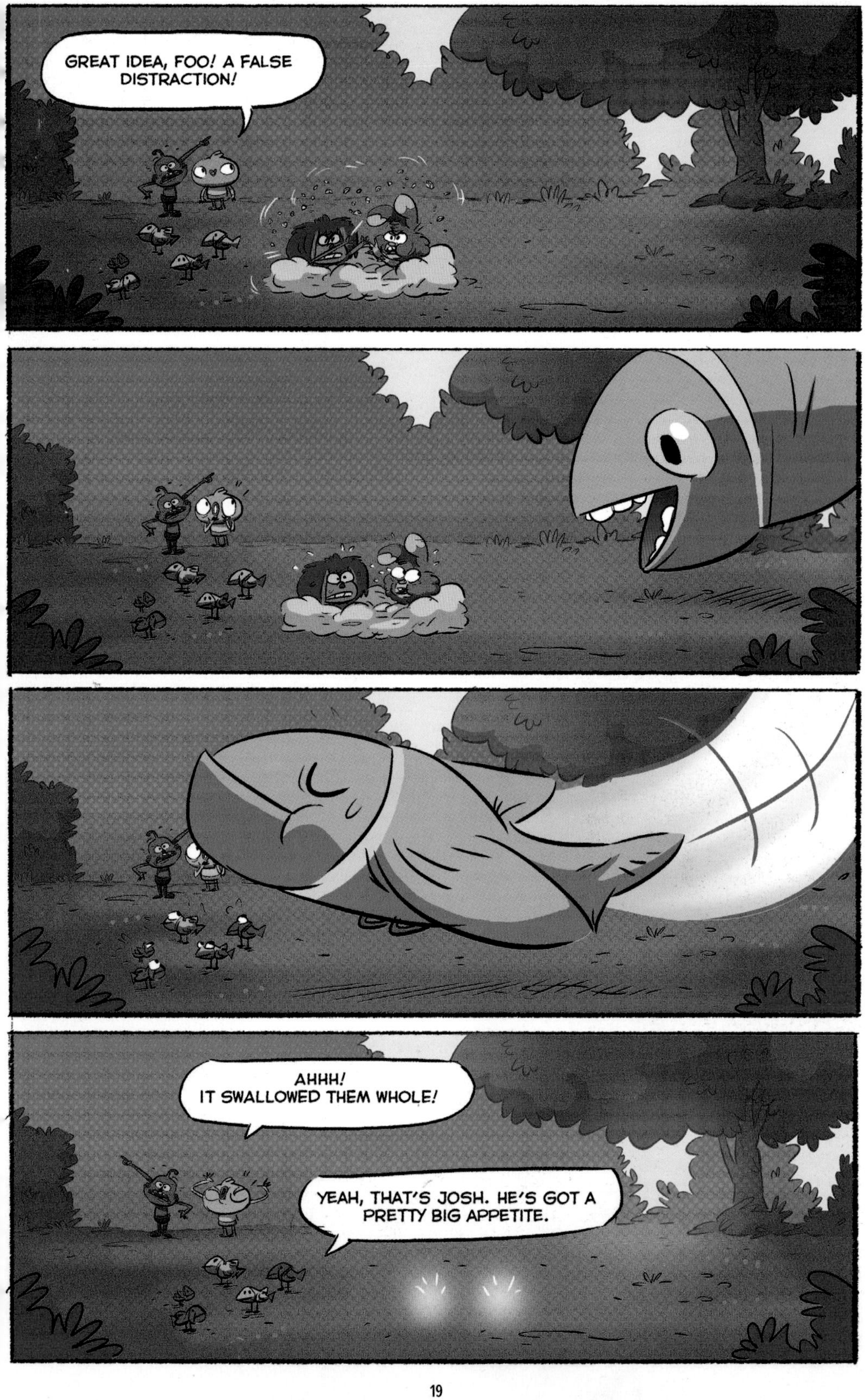
GREAT IDEA, FOO! A FALSE DISTRACTION!
AHHH! IT SWALLOWED THEM WHOLE!
YEAH, THAT'S JOSH. HE'S GOT A PRETTY BIG APPETITE.

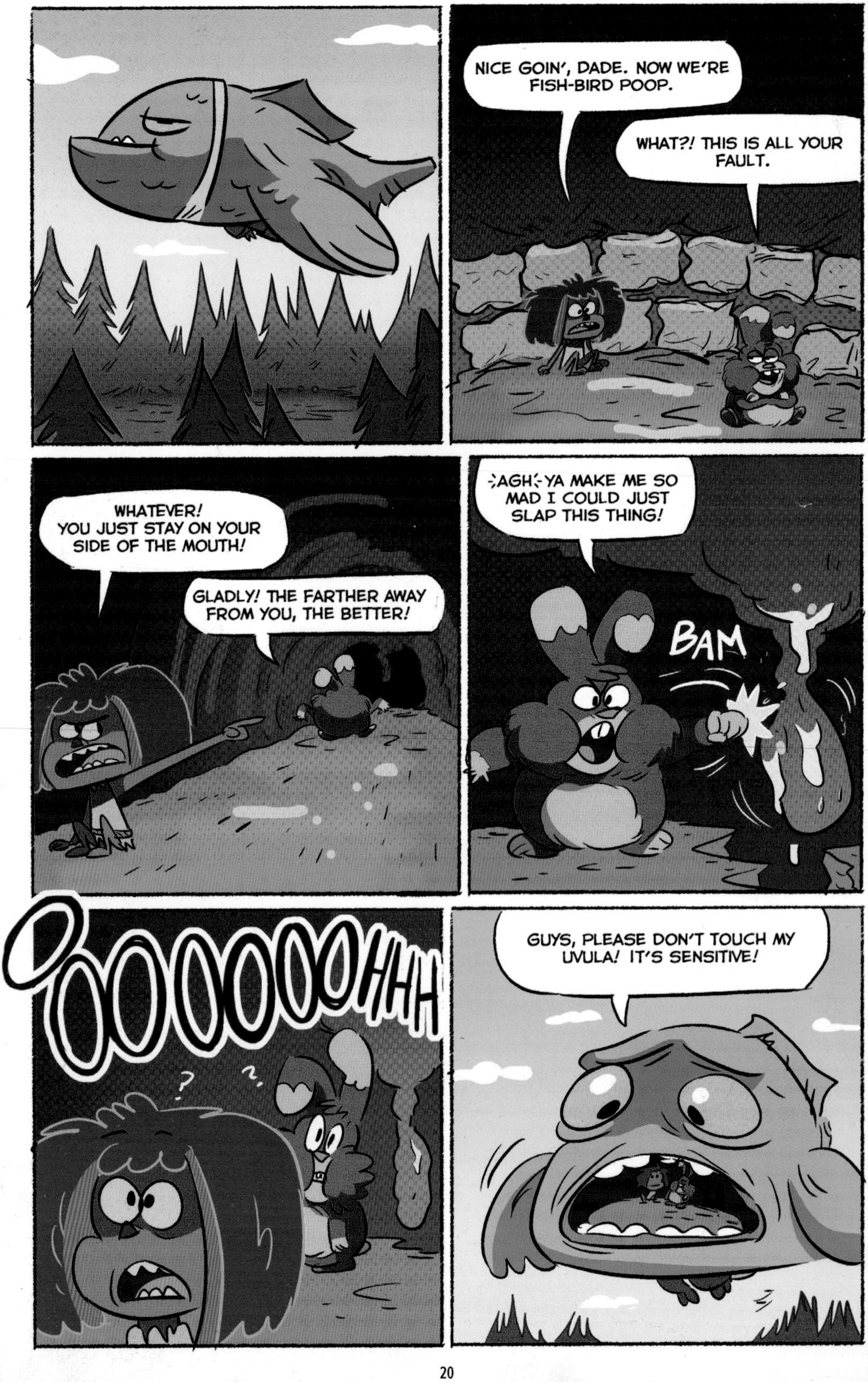
NICE GOIN', DADE. NOW WE'RE FISH-BIRD POOP.
WHAT?! THIS IS ALL YOUR FAULT.
WHATEVER! YOU JUST STAY ON YOUR SIDE OF THE MOUTH!
GLADLY! THE FARTHER AWAY FROM YOU, THE BETTER!
AGH! YA MAKE ME SO MAD I COULD JUST SLAP THIS THING!
BAM
OOOOOOOHHHH
GUYS, PLEASE DON'T TOUCH MY UVULA! IT'S SENSITIVE!

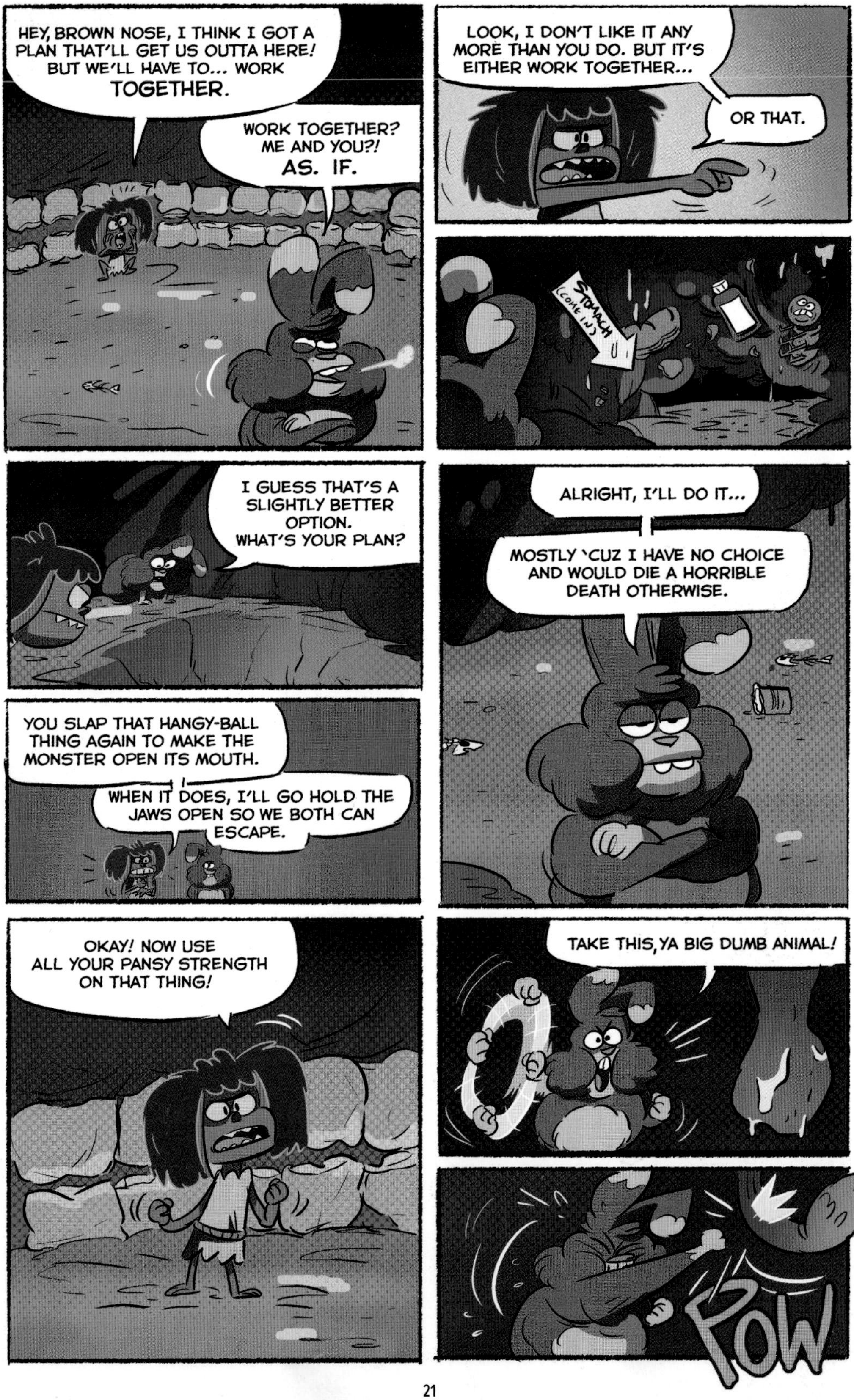
HEY, BROWN NOSE, I THINK I GOT A PLAN THAT'LL GET US OUTTA HERE! BUT WE'LL HAVE TO... WORK TOGETHER.
WORK TOGETHER? ME AND YOU?! AS. IF.
LOOK, I DON'T LIKE IT ANY MORE THAN YOU DO. BUT IT'S EITHER WORK TOGETHER...
OR THAT.
STOMACH (COME IN)
I GUESS THAT'S A SLIGHTLY BETTER OPTION. WHAT'S YOUR PLAN?
YOU SLAP THAT HANGY-BALL THING AGAIN TO MAKE THE MONSTER OPEN ITS MOUTH.
WHEN IT DOES, I'LL GO HOLD THE JAWS OPEN SO WE BOTH CAN ESCAPE.
ALRIGHT, I'LL DO IT...
MOSTLY 'CUZ I HAVE NO CHOICE AND WOULD DIE A HORRIBLE DEATH OTHERWISE.
OKAY! NOW USE ALL YOUR PANSY STRENGTH ON THAT THING!
TAKE THIS, YA BIG DUMB ANIMAL!
POW

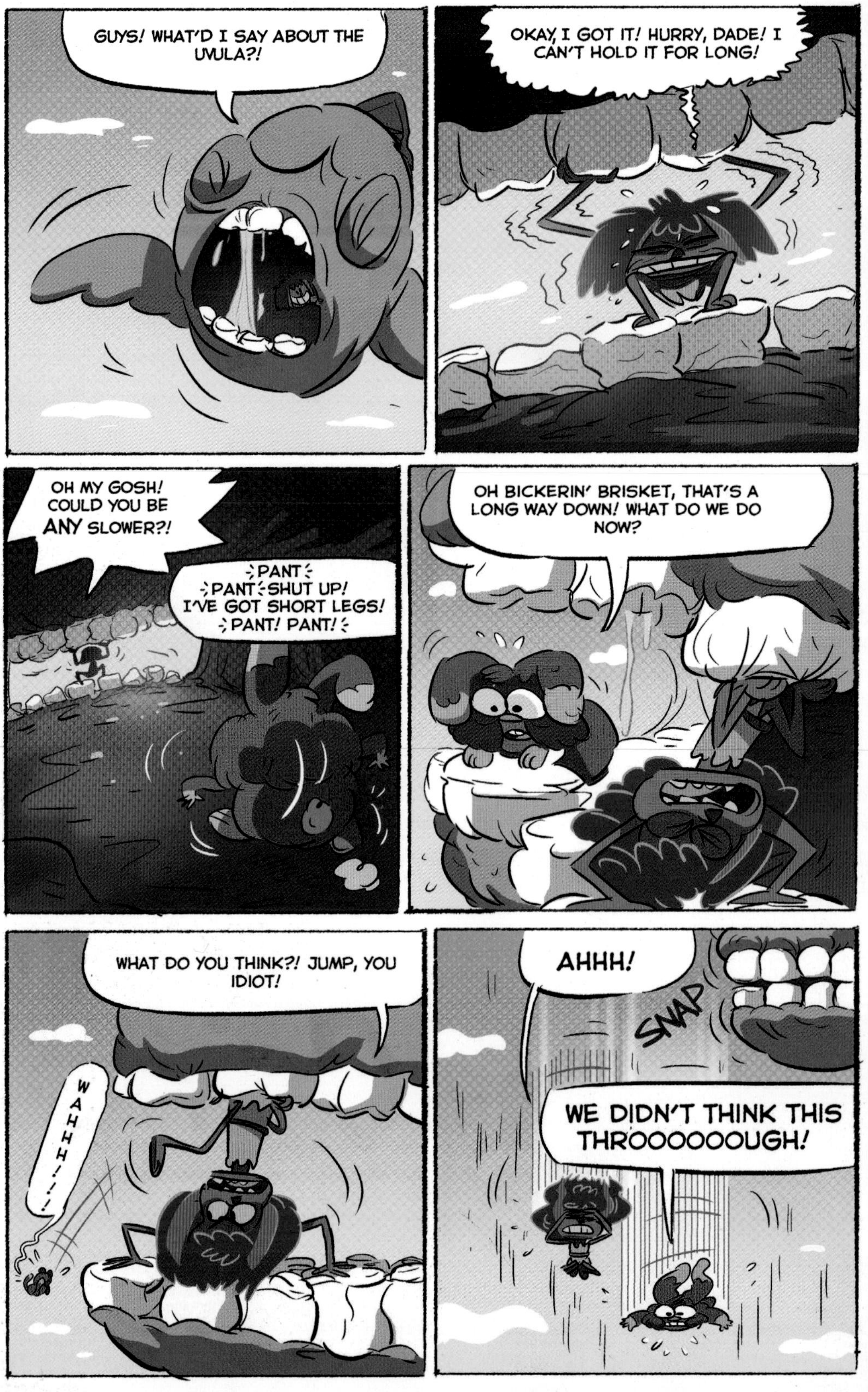
GUYS! WHAT'D I SAY ABOUT THE UVULA?!
OKAY, I GOT IT! HURRY, DADE! I CAN'T HOLD IT FOR LONG!
OH MY GOSH! COULD YOU BE ANY SLOWER?!
PANT PANT SHUT UP! I'VE GOT SHORT LEGS! PANT! PANT!
OH BICKERIN' BRISKET, THAT'S A LONG WAY DOWN! WHAT DO WE DO NOW?
WHAT DO YOU THINK?! JUMP, YOU IDIOT!
WAHHH!!!
AHHH!
SNAP
WE DIDN'T THINK THIS THROOOOOOUGH!

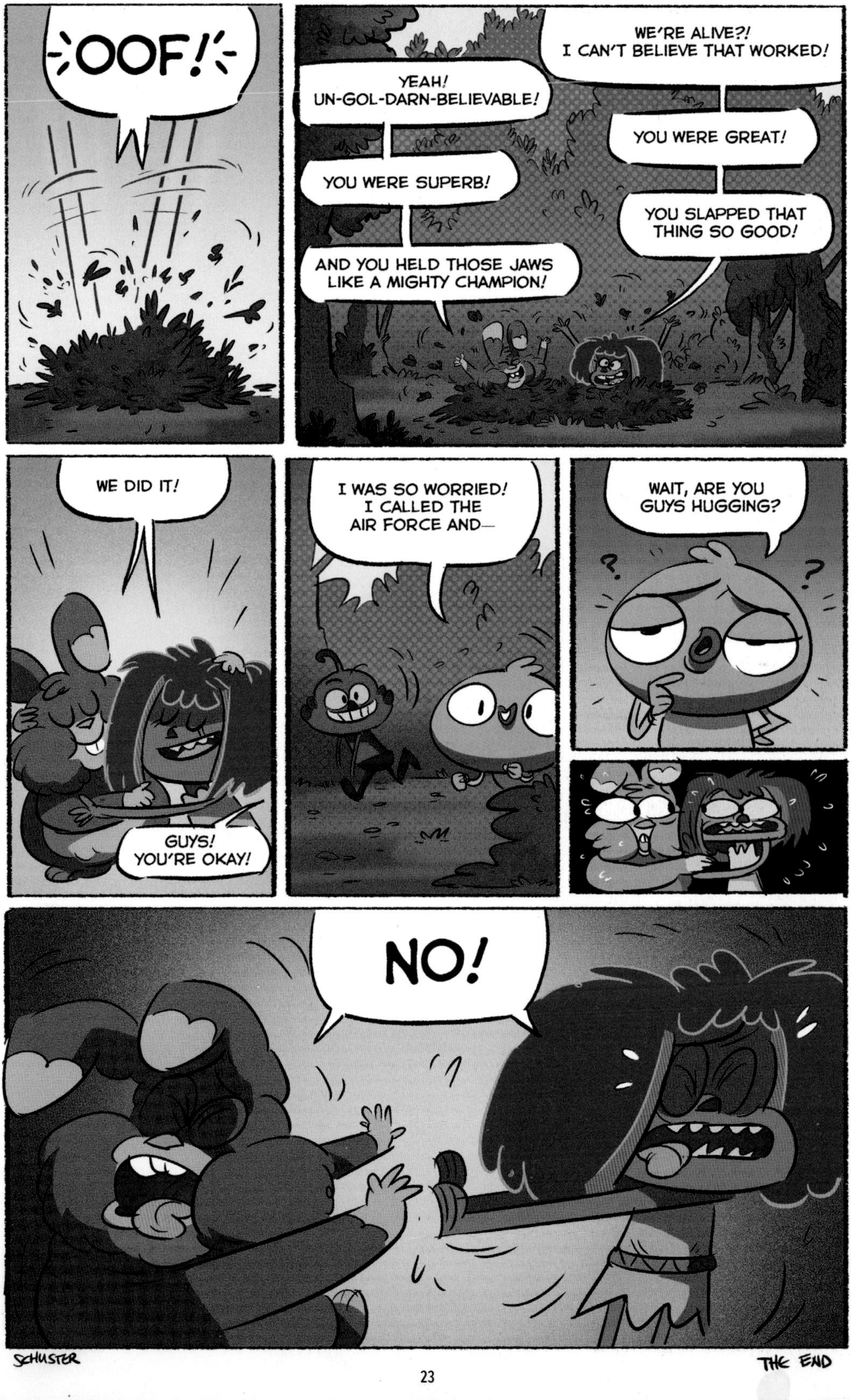
OOF!
WE'RE ALIVE?! I CAN'T BELIEVE THAT WORKED!
YEAH! UN-GOL-DARN-BELIEVABLE!
YOU WERE GREAT!
YOU WERE SUPERB!
YOU SLAPPED THAT THING SO GOOD!
AND YOU HELD THOSE JAWS LIKE A MIGHTY CHAMPION!
WE DID IT!
GUYS! YOU'RE OKAY!
I WAS SO WORRIED! I CALLED THE AIR FORCE AND—
WAIT, ARE YOU GUYS HUGGING?
NO!
SCHUSTER
THE END

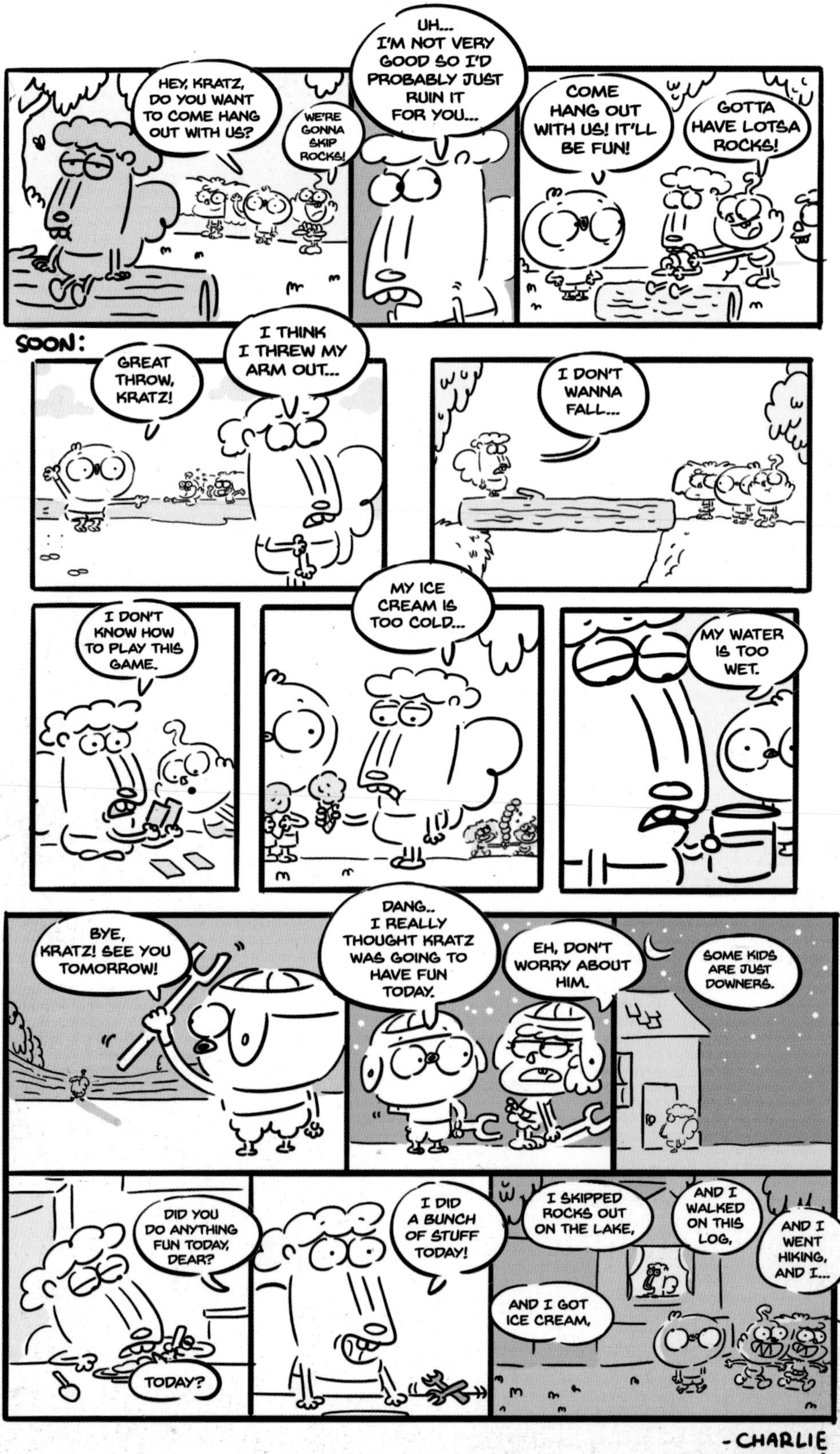
HEY, KRATZ, DO YOU WANT TO COME HANG OUT WITH US?
WE'RE GONNA SKIP ROCKS!
UH... I'M NOT VERY GOOD SO I'D PROBABLY JUST RUIN IT FOR YOU...
COME HANG OUT WITH US! IT'LL BE FUN!
GOTTA HAVE LOTSA ROCKS!
SOON:
GREAT THROW, KRATZ!
I THINK I THREW MY ARM OUT...
I DON'T WANNA FALL...
I DON'T KNOW HOW TO PLAY THIS GAME.
MY ICE CREAM IS TOO COLD...
MY WATER IS TOO WET.
BYE, KRATZ! SEE YOU TOMORROW!
DANG.. I REALLY THOUGHT KRATZ WAS GOING TO HAVE FUN TODAY.
EH, DON'T WORRY ABOUT HIM.
SOME KIDS ARE JUST DOWNERS.
DID YOU DO ANYTHING FUN TODAY, DEAR?
TODAY?
I DID A BUNCH OF STUFF TODAY!
I SKIPPED ROCKS OUT ON THE LAKE,
AND I WALKED ON THIS LOG,
AND I WENT HIKING, AND I...
AND I GOT ICE CREAM,
-CHARLIE GAVIN

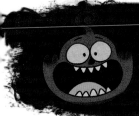

FOO FACT #76 - KETCHUP

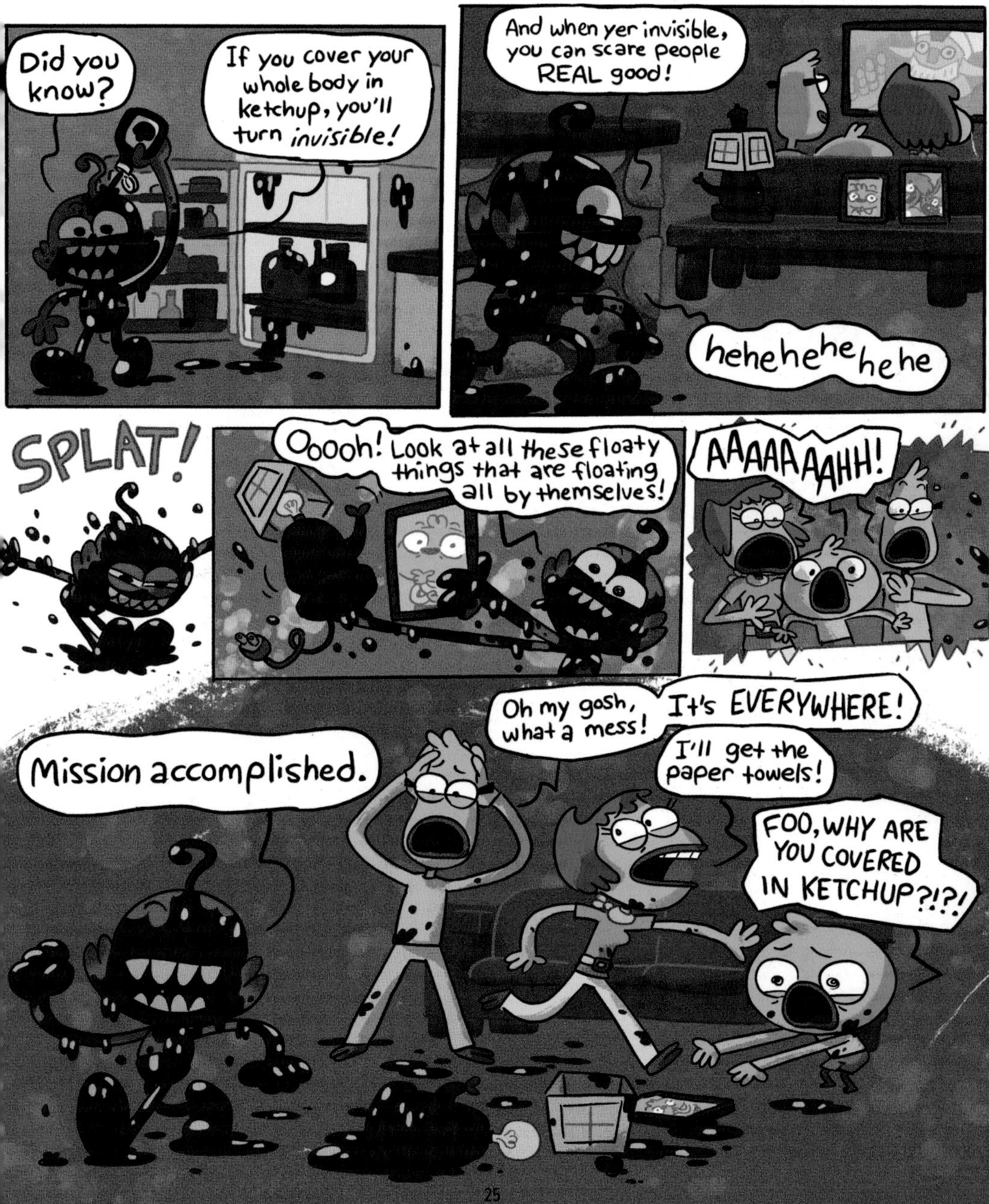

Did you know?
If you cover your whole body in ketchup, you'll turn invisible!
And when yer invisible, you can scare people REAL good!
hehehehehehe
SPLAT!
Ooooh! Look at all these floaty things that are floating all by themselves!
AAAAAAAHH!
Mission accomplished.
Oh my gosh, what a mess!
It's EVERYWHERE!
I'll get the paper towels!
FOO, WHY ARE YOU COVERED IN KETCHUP?!?!

TO DARE OR NOT TO DARE

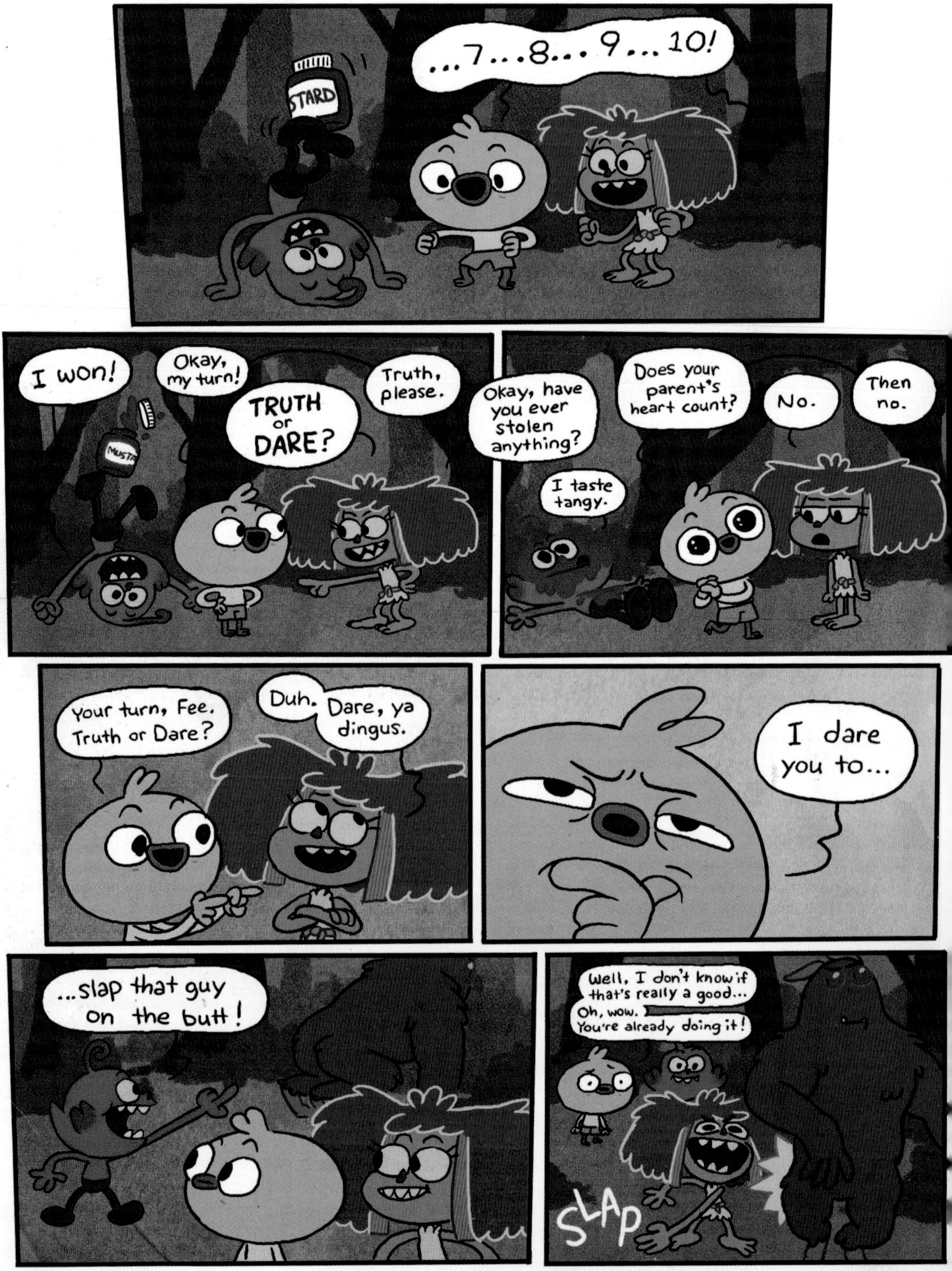

...7...8...9...10!
STARD
I won!
Okay, my turn!
TRUTH or DARE?
Truth, please.
MUSTA
Okay, have you ever stolen anything?
Does your parent's heart count?
No.
Then no.
I taste tangy.
Your turn, Fee. Truth or Dare?
Duh.
Dare, ya dingus.
I dare you to...
...slap that guy on the butt!
Well, I don't know if that's really a good...
Oh, wow.
You're already doing it!
SLAP

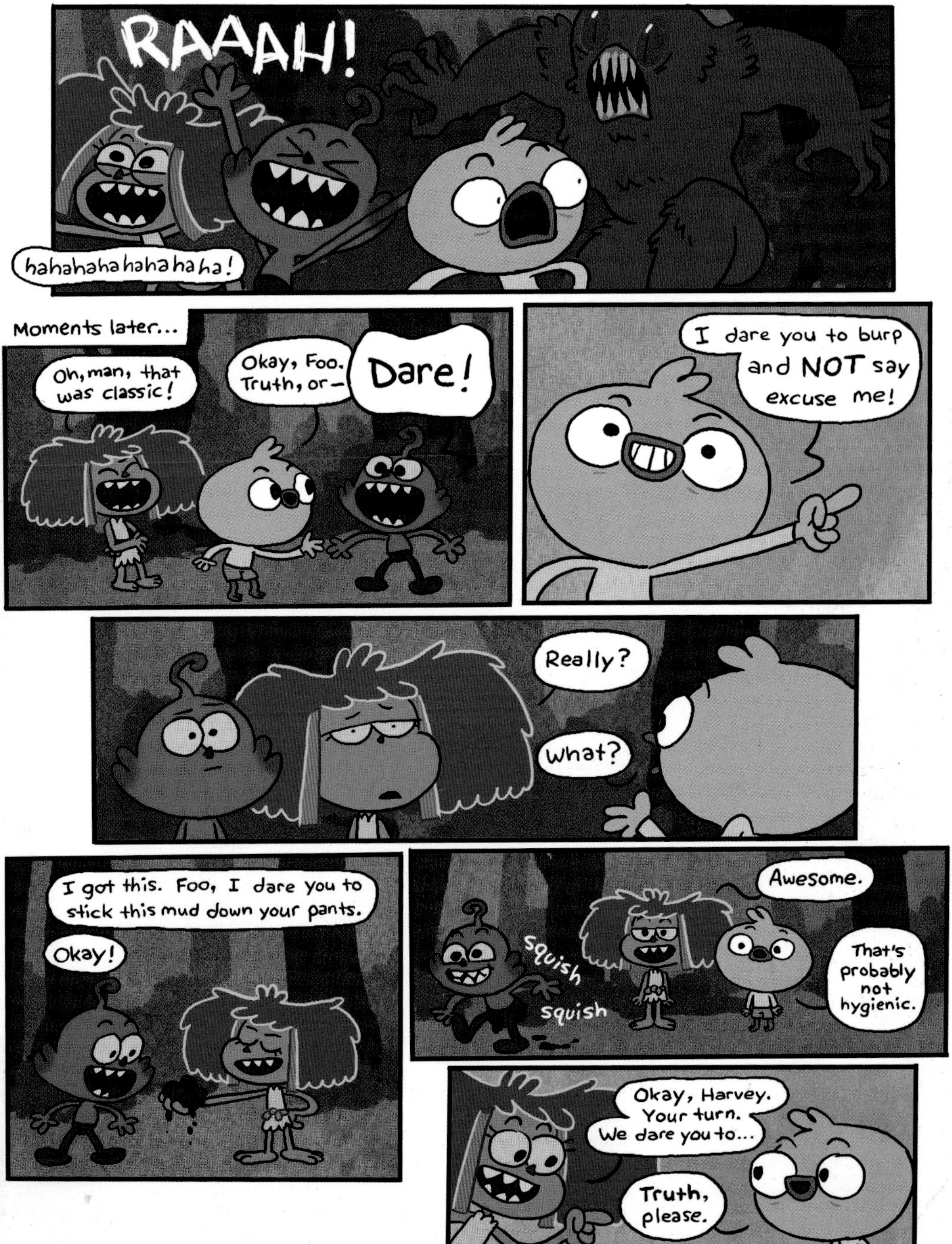
RAAAH!
hahahahahahahaha!
Moments later...
Oh, man, that was classic!
Okay, Foo. Truth, or—
Dare!
I dare you to burp and NOT say excuse me!
Really?
What?
I got this. Foo, I dare you to stick this mud down your pants.
Okay!
squish
squish
Awesome.
That's probably not hygienic.
Okay, Harvey. Your turn. We dare you to...
Truth, please.

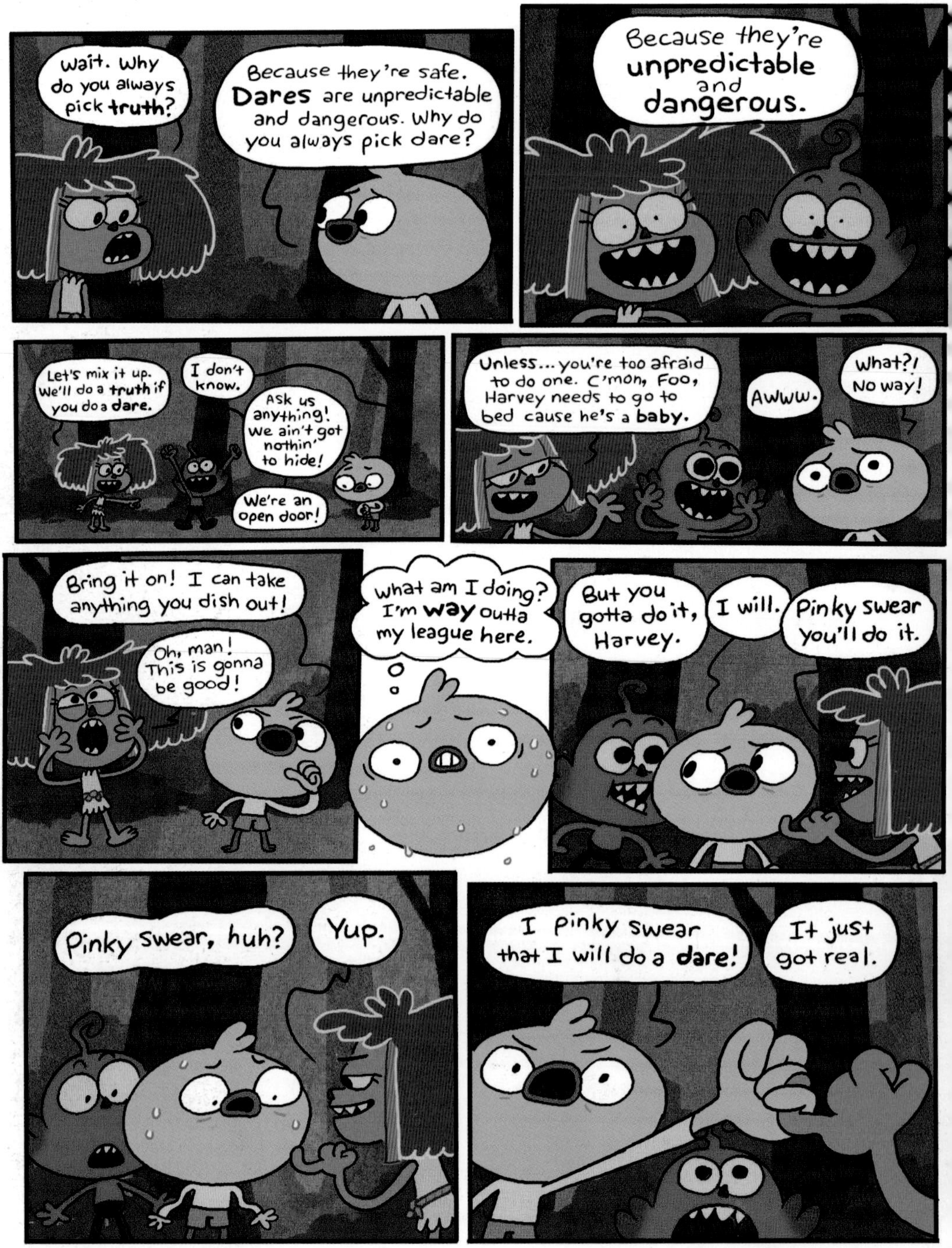
Wait. Why do you always pick truth?
Because they're safe. Dares are unpredictable and dangerous. Why do you always pick dare?
Because they're unpredictable and dangerous.
Let's mix it up. We'll do a truth if you do a dare.
I don't know.
Ask us anything! We ain't got nothin' to hide!
We're an open door!
Unless... you're too afraid to do one. C'mon, Foo, Harvey needs to go to bed cause he's a baby.
AWWW.
What?! No way!
Bring it on! I can take anything you dish out!
Oh, man! This is gonna be good!
What am I doing? I'm way outta my league here.
But you gotta do it, Harvey.
I will.
Pinky swear you'll do it.
Pinky swear, huh?
Yup.
I pinky swear that I will do a dare!
It just got real.

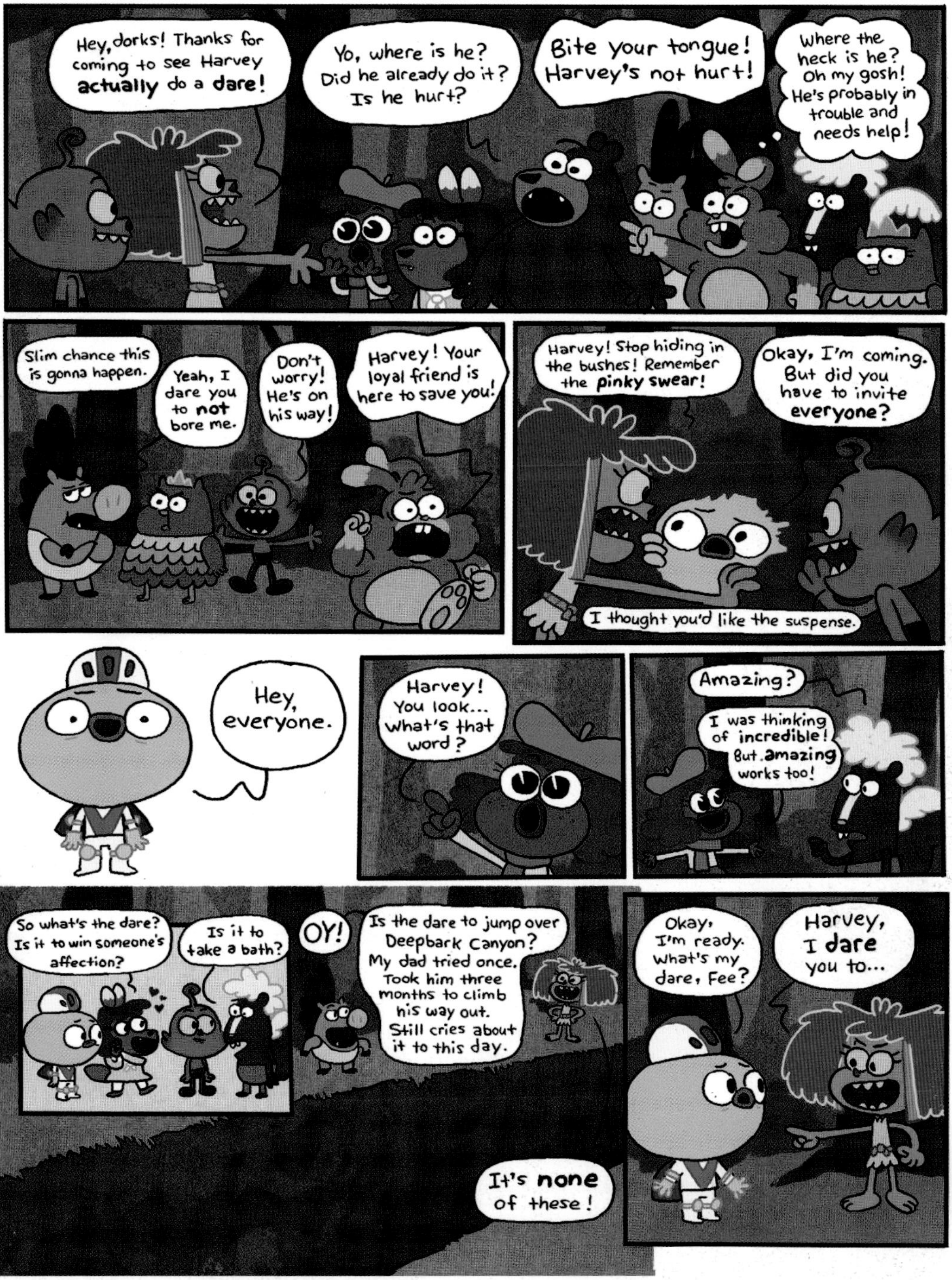

Hey, dorks! Thanks for coming to see Harvey **actually** do a **dare**!
Yo, where is he? Did he already do it? Is he hurt?
Bite your tongue! Harvey's not hurt!
Where the heck is he? Oh my gosh! He's probably in trouble and needs help!
Slim chance this is gonna happen.
Yeah, I dare you to **not** bore me.
Don't worry! He's on his way!
Harvey! Your loyal friend is here to save you!
Harvey! Stop hiding in the bushes! Remember the **pinky swear**!
Okay, I'm coming. But did you have to invite **everyone?**
I thought you'd like the suspense.
Hey, everyone.
Harvey! You look... what's that word?
Amazing?
I was thinking of **incredible**! But **amazing** works too!
So what's the dare? Is it to win someone's affection?
Is it to take a bath?
OY!
Is the dare to jump over Deepbark Canyon? My dad tried once. Took him three months to climb his way out. Still cries about it to this day.
It's **none** of these!
Okay, I'm ready. What's my dare, Fee?
Harvey, I **dare** you to...

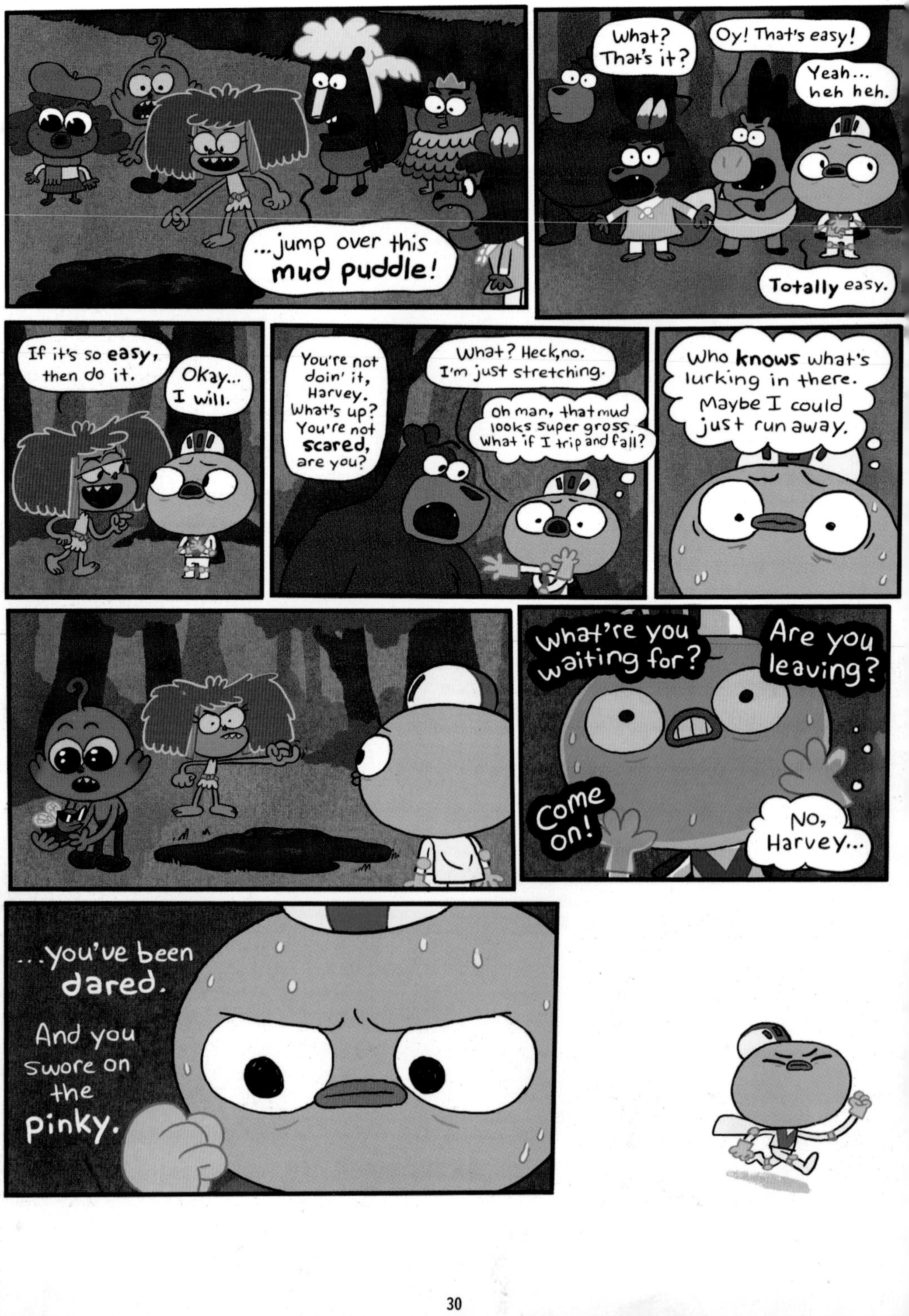
...jump over this mud puddle!
What? That's it?
Oy! That's easy!
Yeah... heh heh.
Totally easy.
If it's so easy, then do it.
Okay... I will.
You're not doin' it, Harvey. What's up? You're not scared, are you?
What? Heck, no. I'm just stretching.
Oh man, that mud looks super gross. What if I trip and fall?
Who knows what's lurking in there. Maybe I could just run away.
What're you waiting for?
Are you leaving?
Come on!
No, Harvey...
...you've been dared.
And you swore on the pinky.

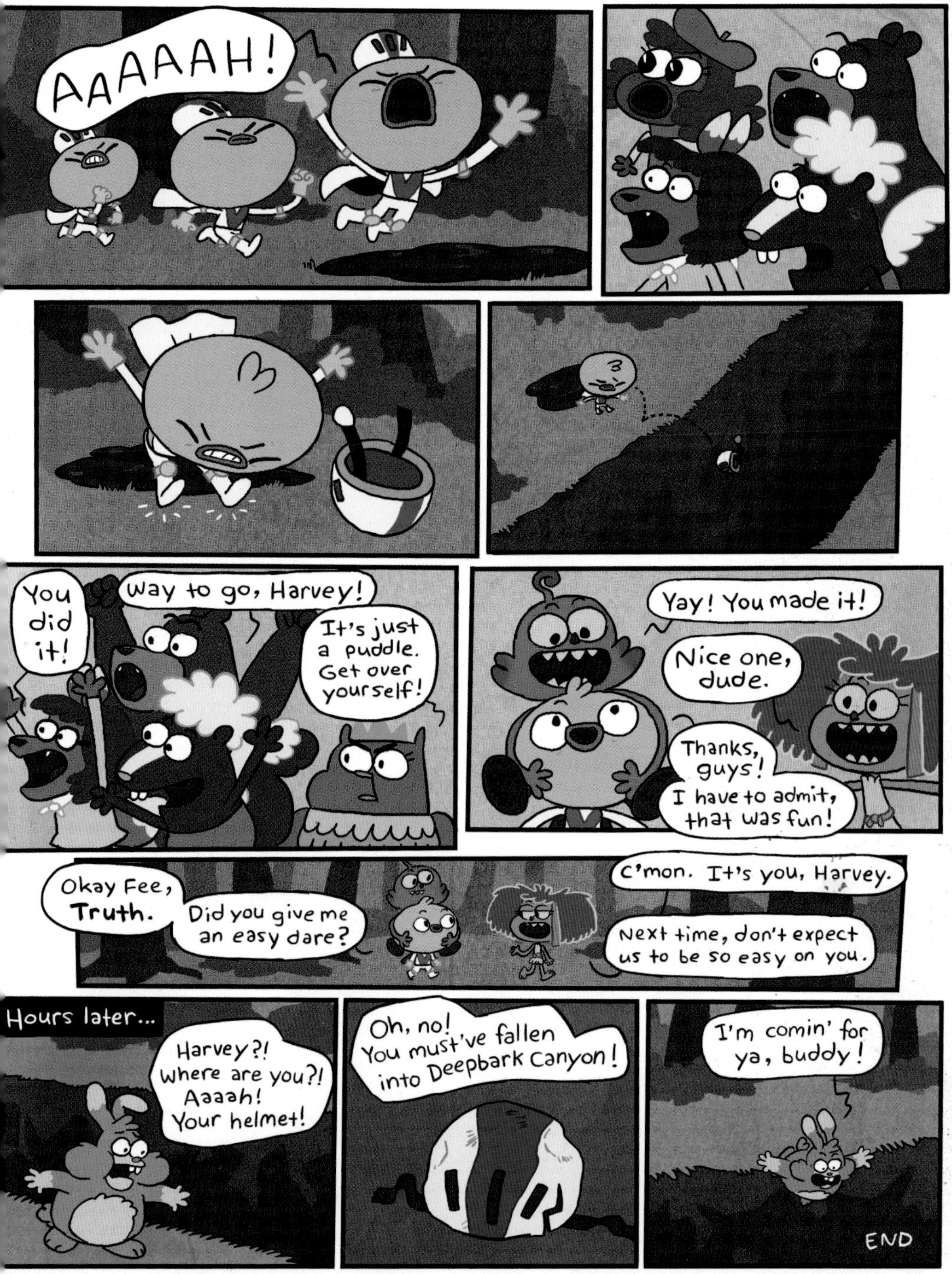
AAAAAH!
You did it!
Way to go, Harvey!
It's just a puddle. Get over yourself!
Yay! You made it!
Nice one, dude.
Thanks, guys!
I have to admit, that was fun!
Okay Fee, Truth.
Did you give me an easy dare?
C'mon. It's you, Harvey.
Next time, don't expect us to be so easy on you.
Hours later...
Harvey?! Where are you?! Aaaah! Your helmet!
Oh, no! You must've fallen into Deepbark Canyon!
I'm comin' for ya, buddy!
END

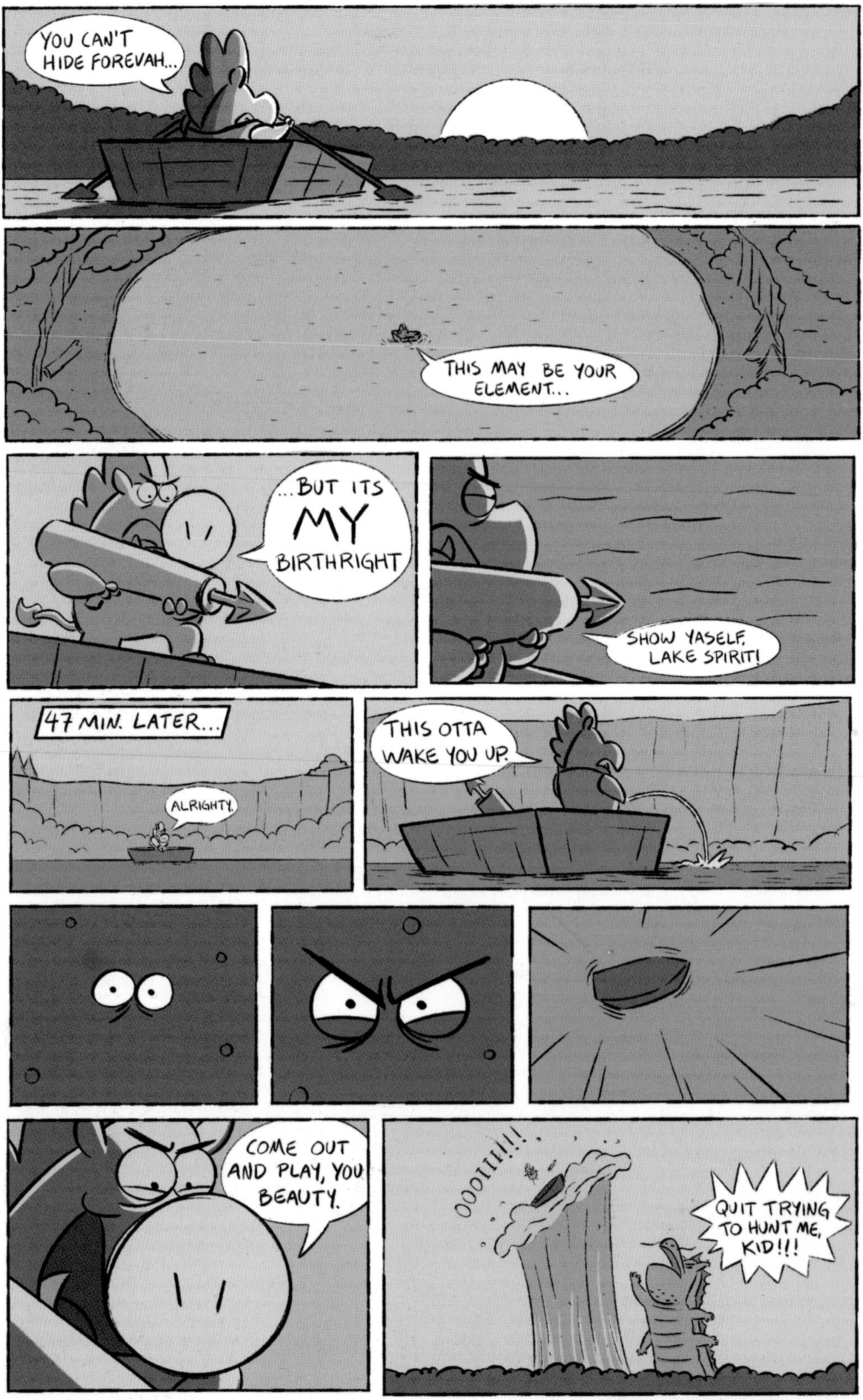
YOU CAN'T HIDE FOREVAH...
THIS MAY BE YOUR ELEMENT...
...BUT ITS MY BIRTHRIGHT
SHOW YASELF, LAKE SPIRIT!
47 MIN. LATER...
ALRIGHTY.
THIS OTTA WAKE YOU UP.
COME OUT AND PLAY, YOU BEAUTY.
OOOIIII!!!
QUIT TRYING TO HUNT ME, KID!!!

CELESTINO MARINA

THE MOST DANGEROUS GAME

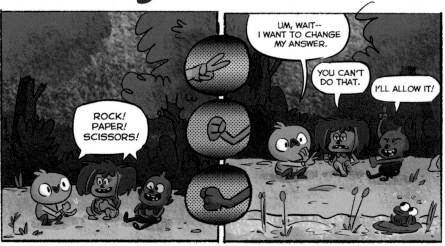

ROCK! PAPER! SCISSORS!

UM, WAIT-- I WANT TO CHANGE MY ANSWER.

YOU CAN'T DO THAT.

I'LL ALLOW IT!

SCISSORS CAN BE PRETTY DANGEROUS. I DON'T THINK IT'S A GOOD IDEA FOR ME TO BE THROWING THESE AROUND WILLY-NILLY.

I'LL GO PAPER--

NO, WAIT! I FORGOT ABOUT PAPER CUTS!

WHAT'S THE BIG DEAL ABOUT SCISSORS AND PAPER? YOU USE THOSE THINGS ALL THE TIME!

ONLY WHEN CRAFTING. BUT I'VE NEVER USED THEM AGAINST SOMEONE.

I MEAN, JUST IMAGINE...

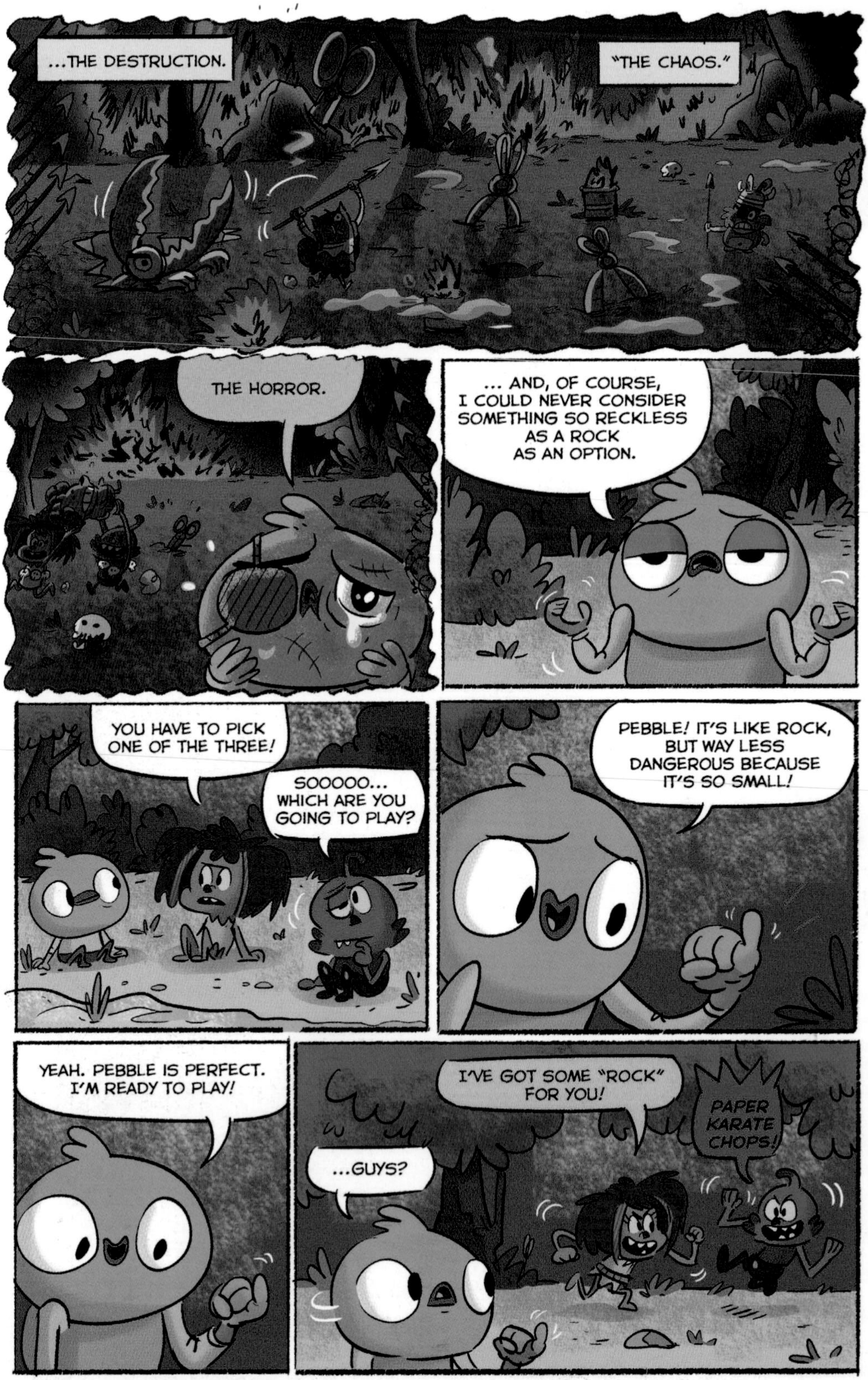
...THE DESTRUCTION.
"THE CHAOS."
THE HORROR.
... AND, OF COURSE, I COULD NEVER CONSIDER SOMETHING SO RECKLESS AS A ROCK AS AN OPTION.
YOU HAVE TO PICK ONE OF THE THREE!
SOOOOO... WHICH ARE YOU GOING TO PLAY?
PEBBLE! IT'S LIKE ROCK, BUT WAY LESS DANGEROUS BECAUSE IT'S SO SMALL!
YEAH. PEBBLE IS PERFECT. I'M READY TO PLAY!
I'VE GOT SOME "ROCK" FOR YOU!
PAPER KARATE CHOPS!
...GUYS?

Harvey Beaks FOOGITIVES

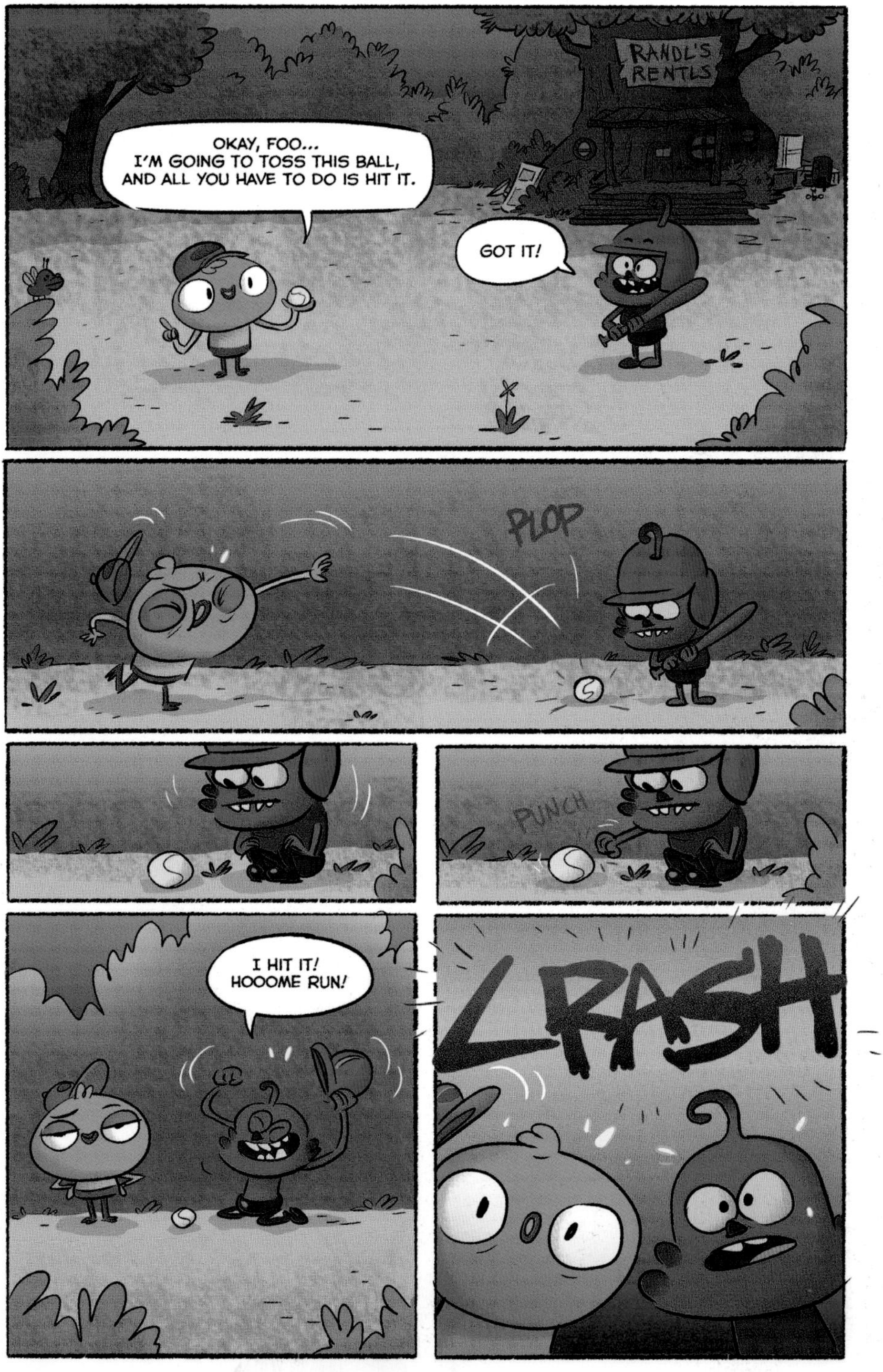
RANDL'S RENTLS
OKAY, FOO... I'M GOING TO TOSS THIS BALL, AND ALL YOU HAVE TO DO IS HIT IT.
GOT IT!
PLOP
PUNCH
I HIT IT! HOOOME RUN!
CRASH

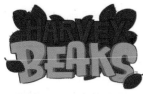

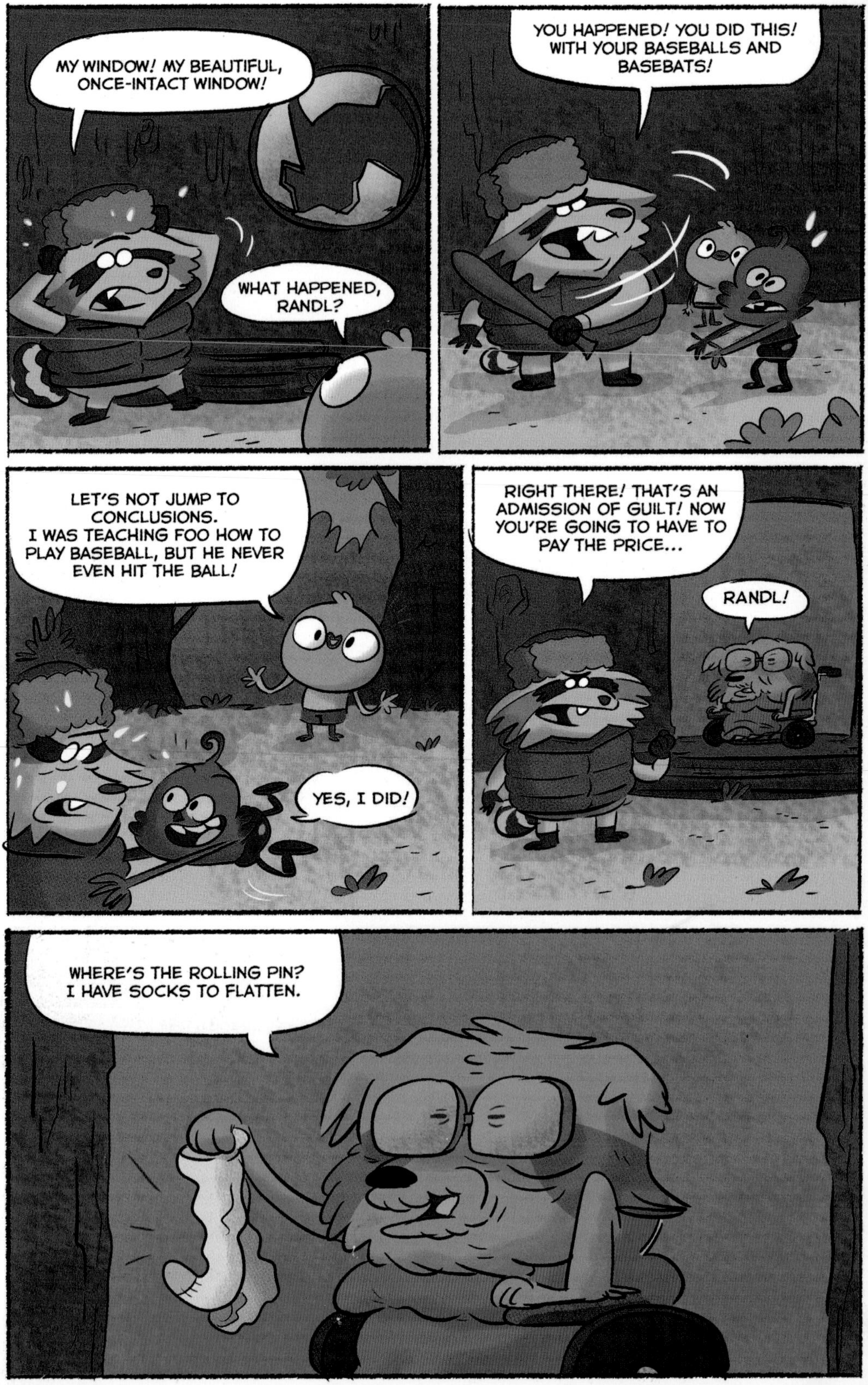
MY WINDOW! MY BEAUTIFUL, ONCE-INTACT WINDOW!
WHAT HAPPENED, RANDL?
YOU HAPPENED! YOU DID THIS! WITH YOUR BASEBALLS AND BASEBATS!
LET'S NOT JUMP TO CONCLUSIONS. I WAS TEACHING FOO HOW TO PLAY BASEBALL, BUT HE NEVER EVEN HIT THE BALL!
YES, I DID!
RIGHT THERE! THAT'S AN ADMISSION OF GUILT! NOW YOU'RE GOING TO HAVE TO PAY THE PRICE...
RANDL!
WHERE'S THE ROLLING PIN? I HAVE SOCKS TO FLATTEN.

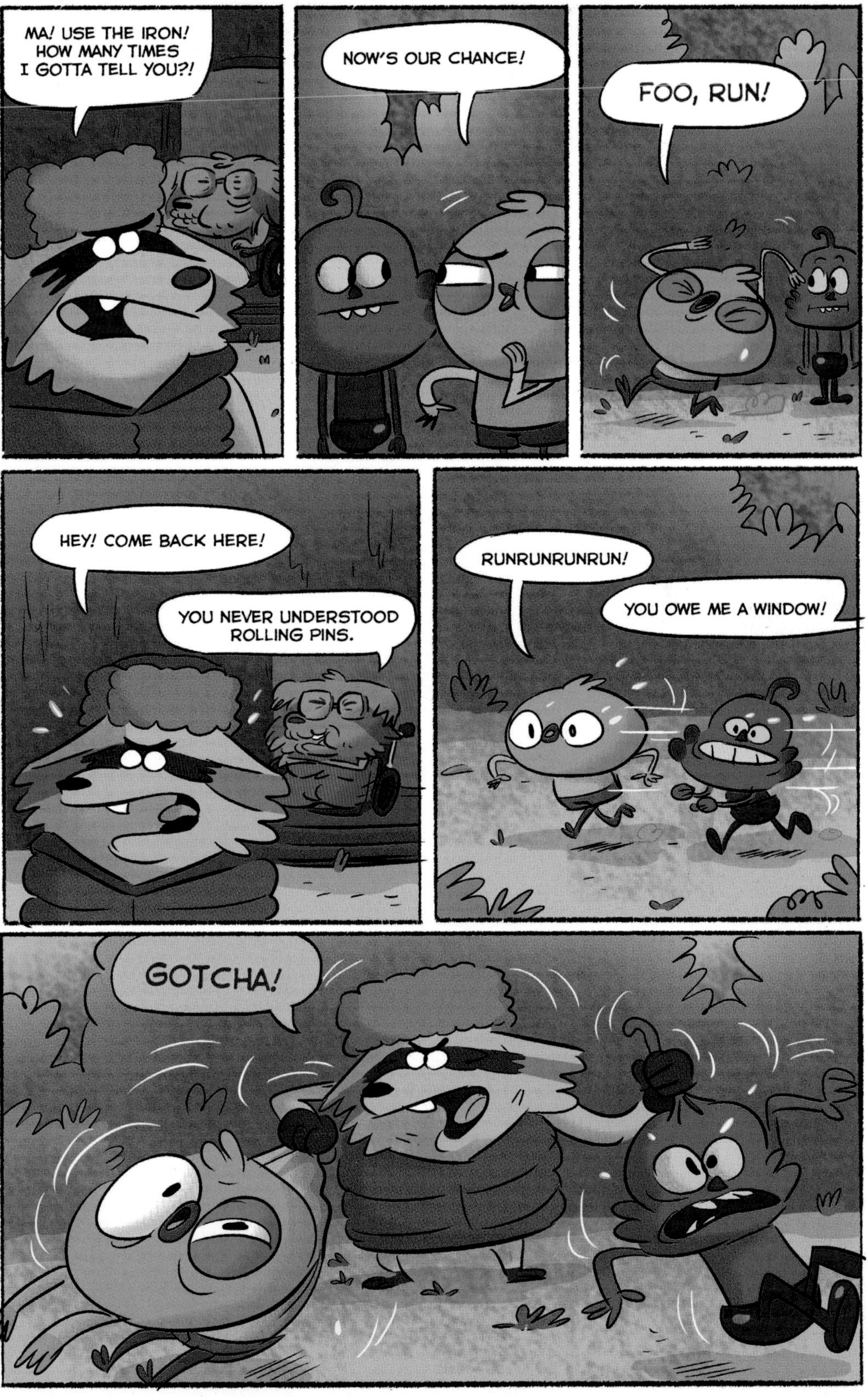
MA! USE THE IRON! HOW MANY TIMES I GOTTA TELL YOU?!
NOW'S OUR CHANCE!
FOO, RUN!
HEY! COME BACK HERE!
YOU NEVER UNDERSTOOD ROLLING PINS.
RUNRUNRUNRUN!
YOU OWE ME A WINDOW!
GOTCHA!

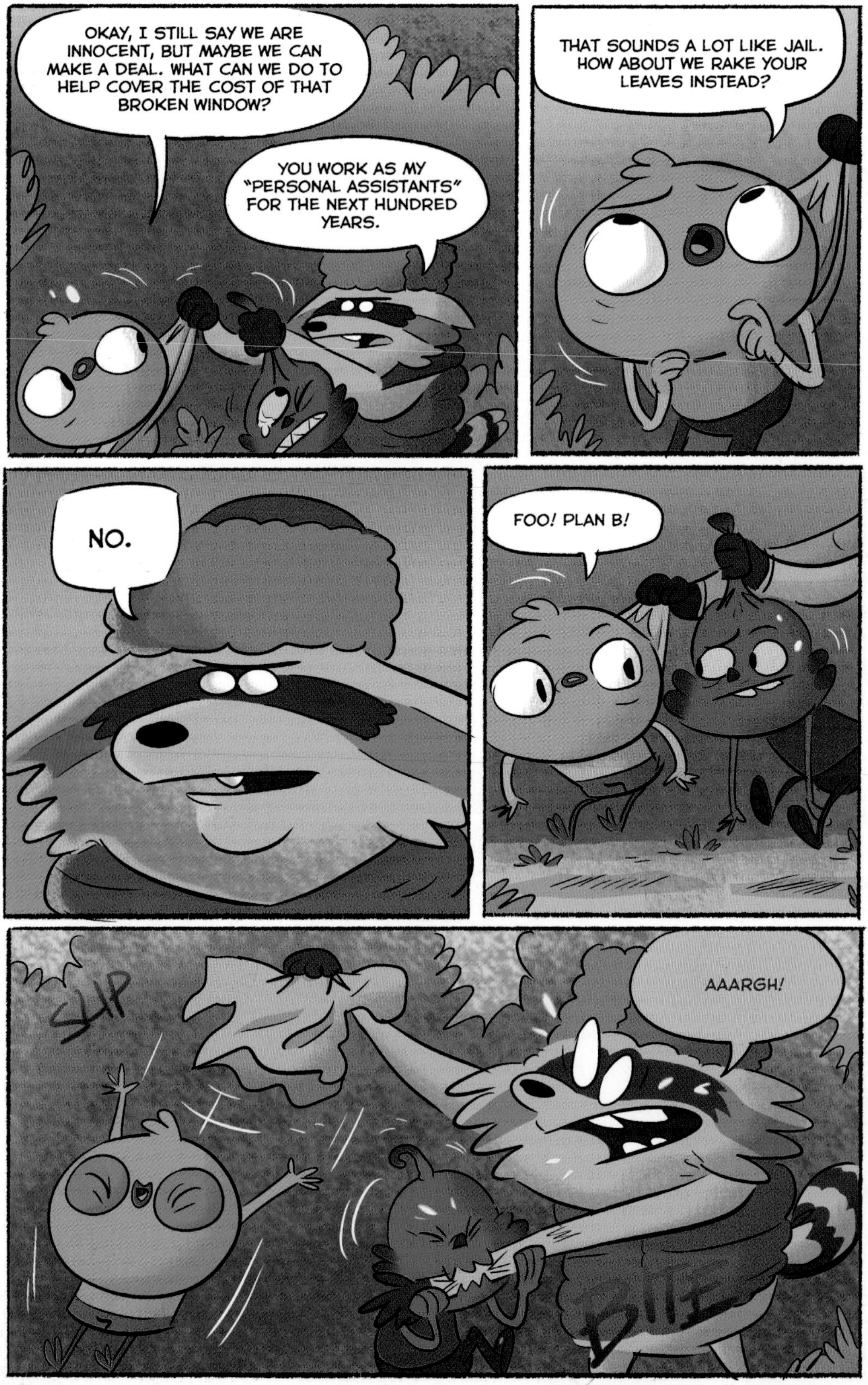
OKAY, I STILL SAY WE ARE INNOCENT, BUT MAYBE WE CAN MAKE A DEAL. WHAT CAN WE DO TO HELP COVER THE COST OF THAT BROKEN WINDOW?
YOU WORK AS MY "PERSONAL ASSISTANTS" FOR THE NEXT HUNDRED YEARS.
THAT SOUNDS A LOT LIKE JAIL. HOW ABOUT WE RAKE YOUR LEAVES INSTEAD?
NO.
FOO! PLAN B!
SLIP
AAARGH!

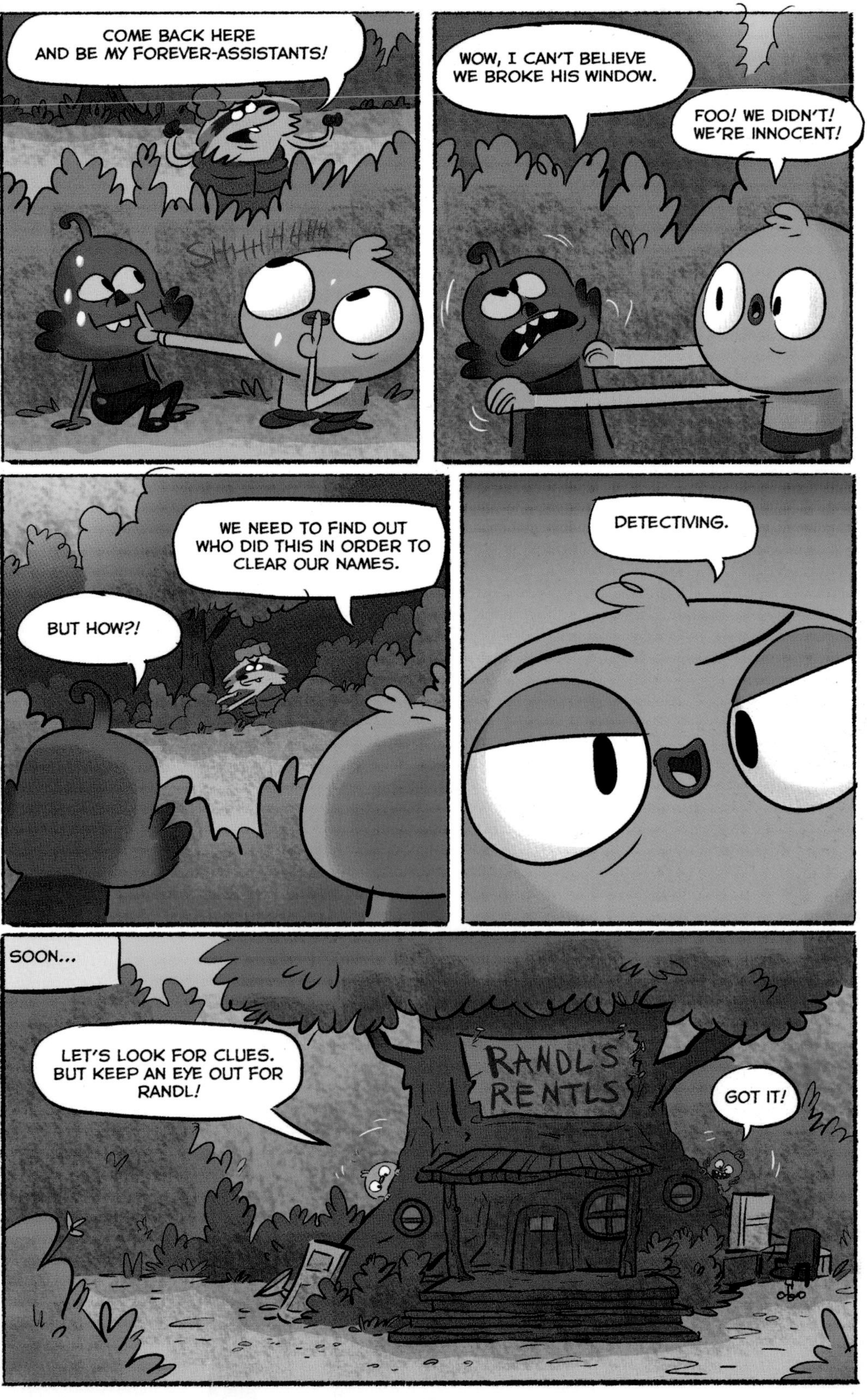
COME BACK HERE AND BE MY FOREVER-ASSISTANTS!
SHHHHHHH
WOW, I CAN'T BELIEVE WE BROKE HIS WINDOW.
FOO! WE DIDN'T! WE'RE INNOCENT!
WE NEED TO FIND OUT WHO DID THIS IN ORDER TO CLEAR OUR NAMES.
BUT HOW?!
DETECTIVING.
SOON...
LET'S LOOK FOR CLUES. BUT KEEP AN EYE OUT FOR RANDL!
RANDL'S RENTLS
GOT IT!

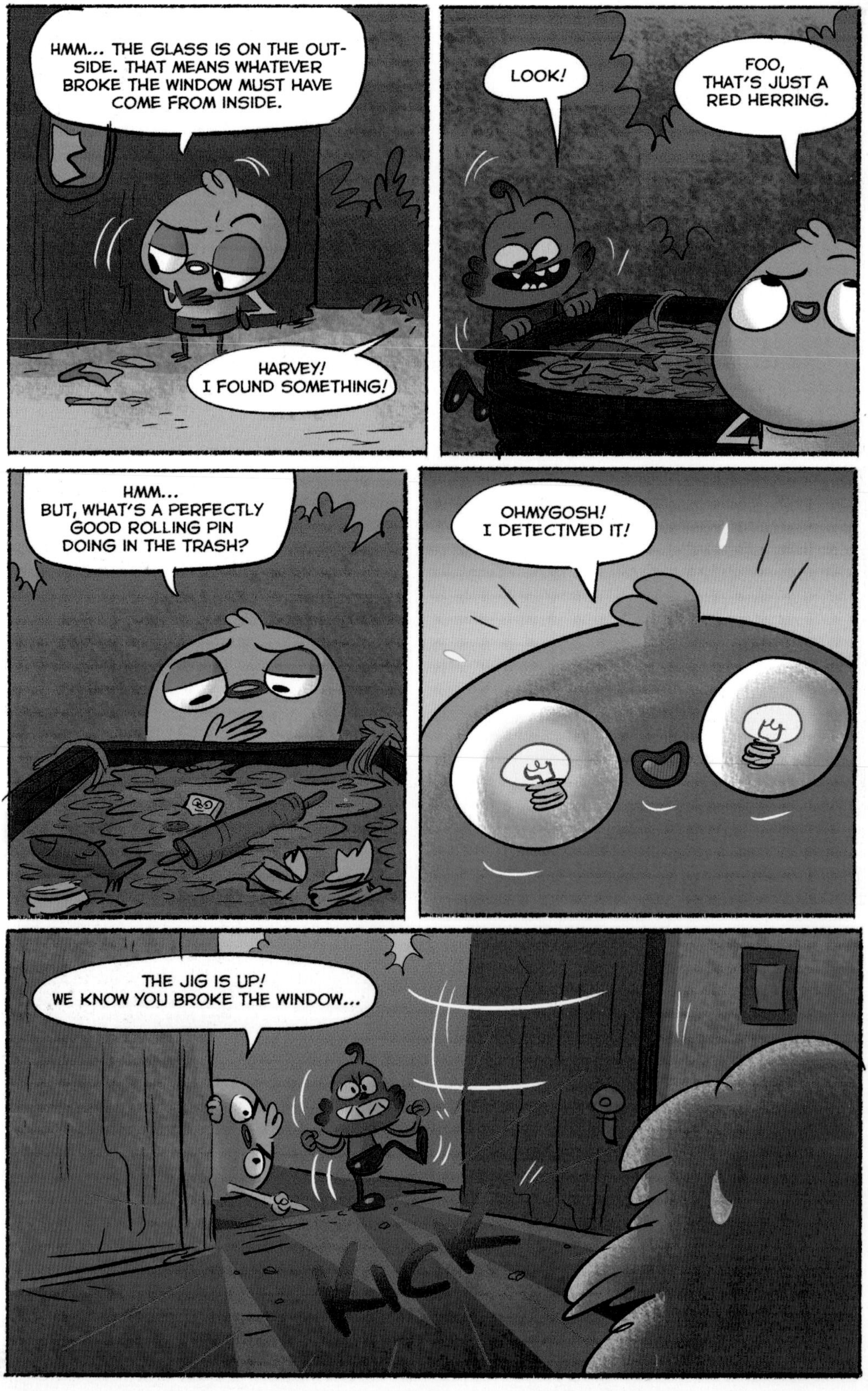
HMM... THE GLASS IS ON THE OUT-SIDE. THAT MEANS WHATEVER BROKE THE WINDOW MUST HAVE COME FROM INSIDE.
HARVEY! I FOUND SOMETHING!
LOOK!
FOO, THAT'S JUST A RED HERRING.
HMM... BUT, WHAT'S A PERFECTLY GOOD ROLLING PIN DOING IN THE TRASH?
OHMYGOSH! I DETECTIVED IT!
THE JIG IS UP! WE KNOW YOU BROKE THE WINDOW...
KICK

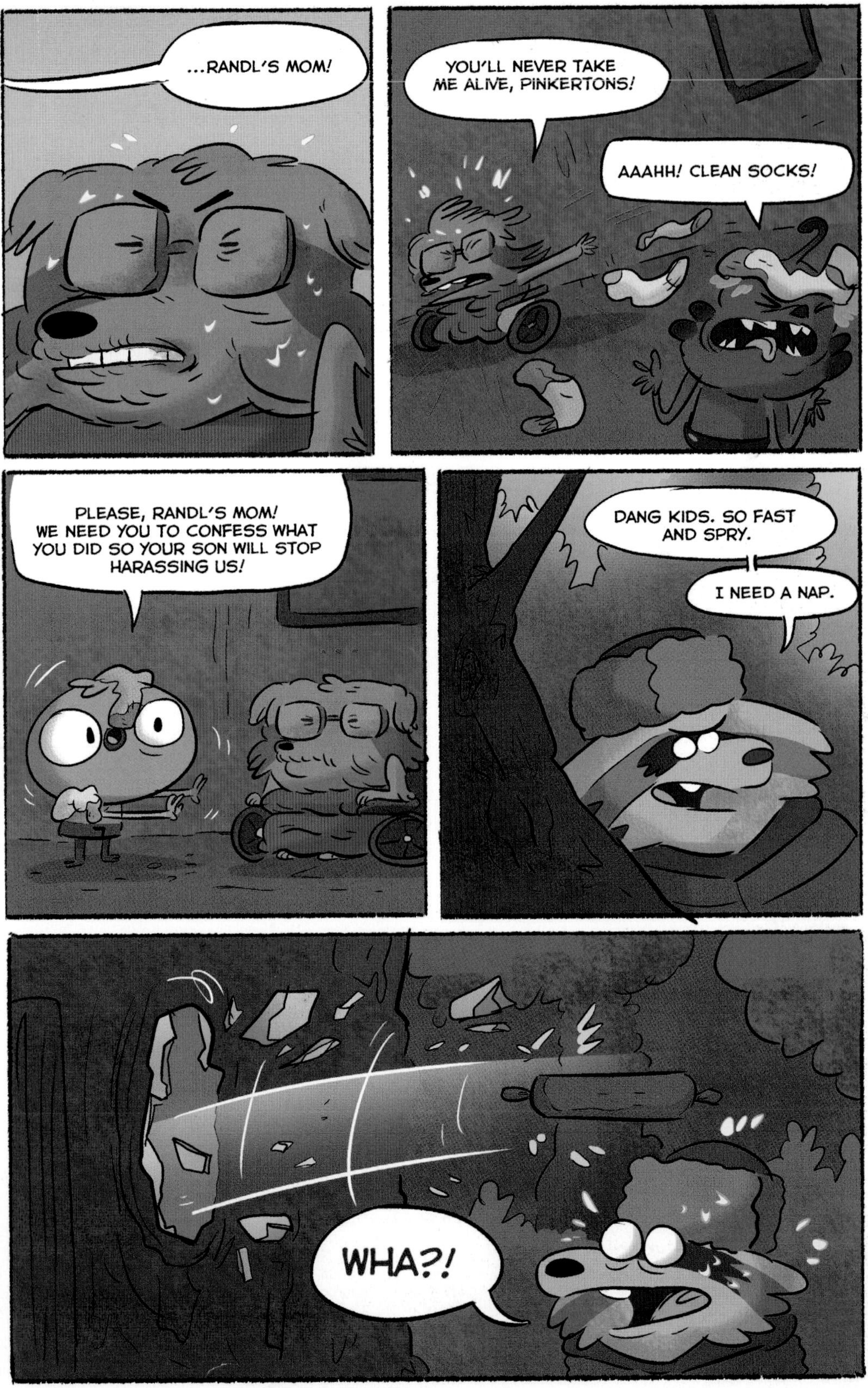
...RANDL'S MOM!
YOU'LL NEVER TAKE ME ALIVE, PINKERTONS!
AAAHH! CLEAN SOCKS!
PLEASE, RANDL'S MOM! WE NEED YOU TO CONFESS WHAT YOU DID SO YOUR SON WILL STOP HARASSING US!
DANG KIDS. SO FAST AND SPRY.
I NEED A NAP.
WHA?!

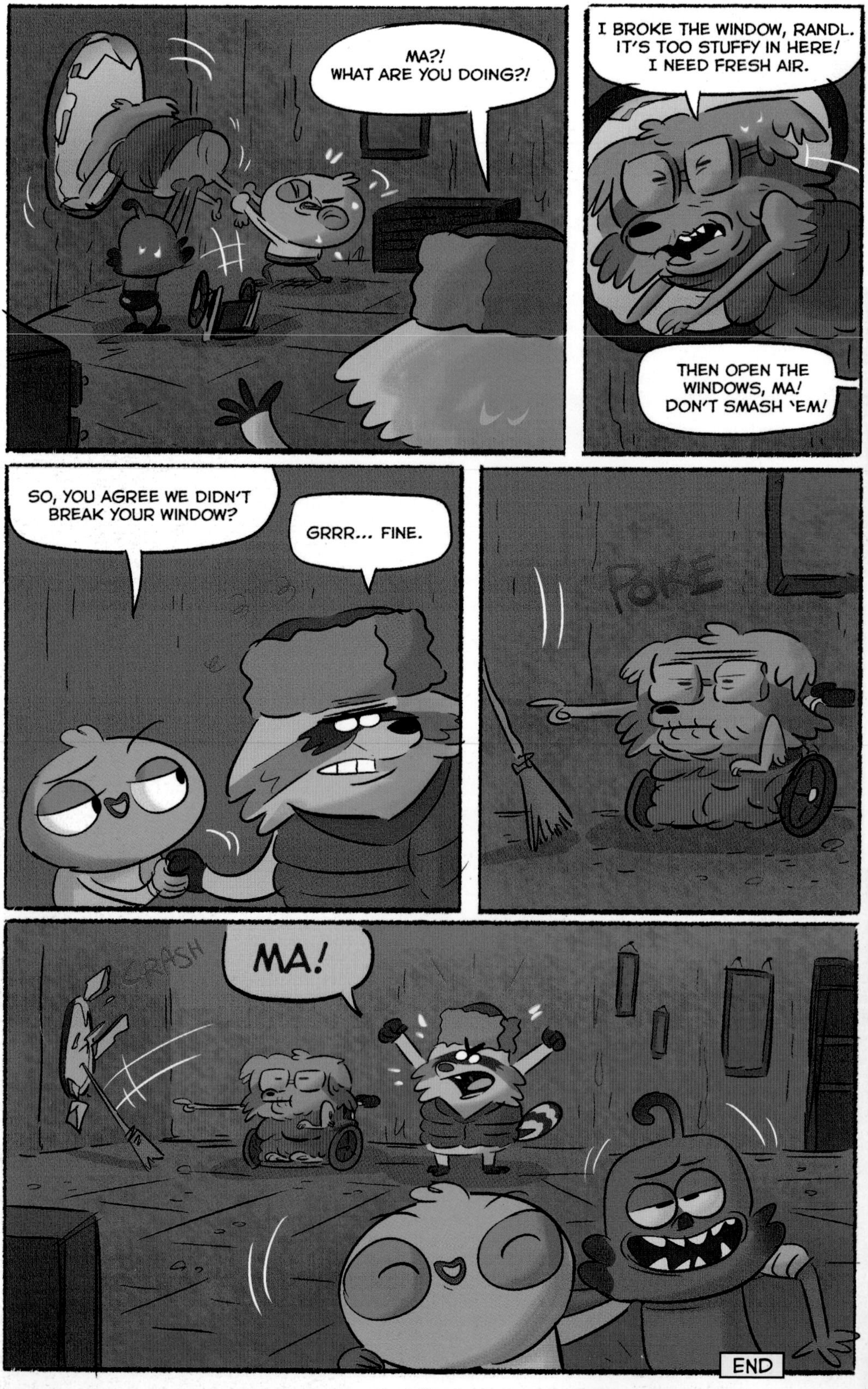
MA?! WHAT ARE YOU DOING?!
I BROKE THE WINDOW, RANDL. IT'S TOO STUFFY IN HERE! I NEED FRESH AIR.
THEN OPEN THE WINDOWS, MA! DON'T SMASH 'EM!
SO, YOU AGREE WE DIDN'T BREAK YOUR WINDOW?
GRRR... FINE.
POKE
CRASH
MA!
END

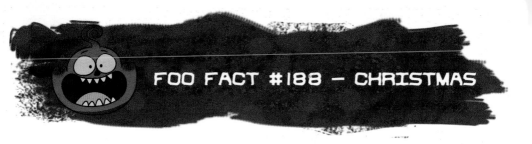

FOO FACT #188 - CHRISTMAS

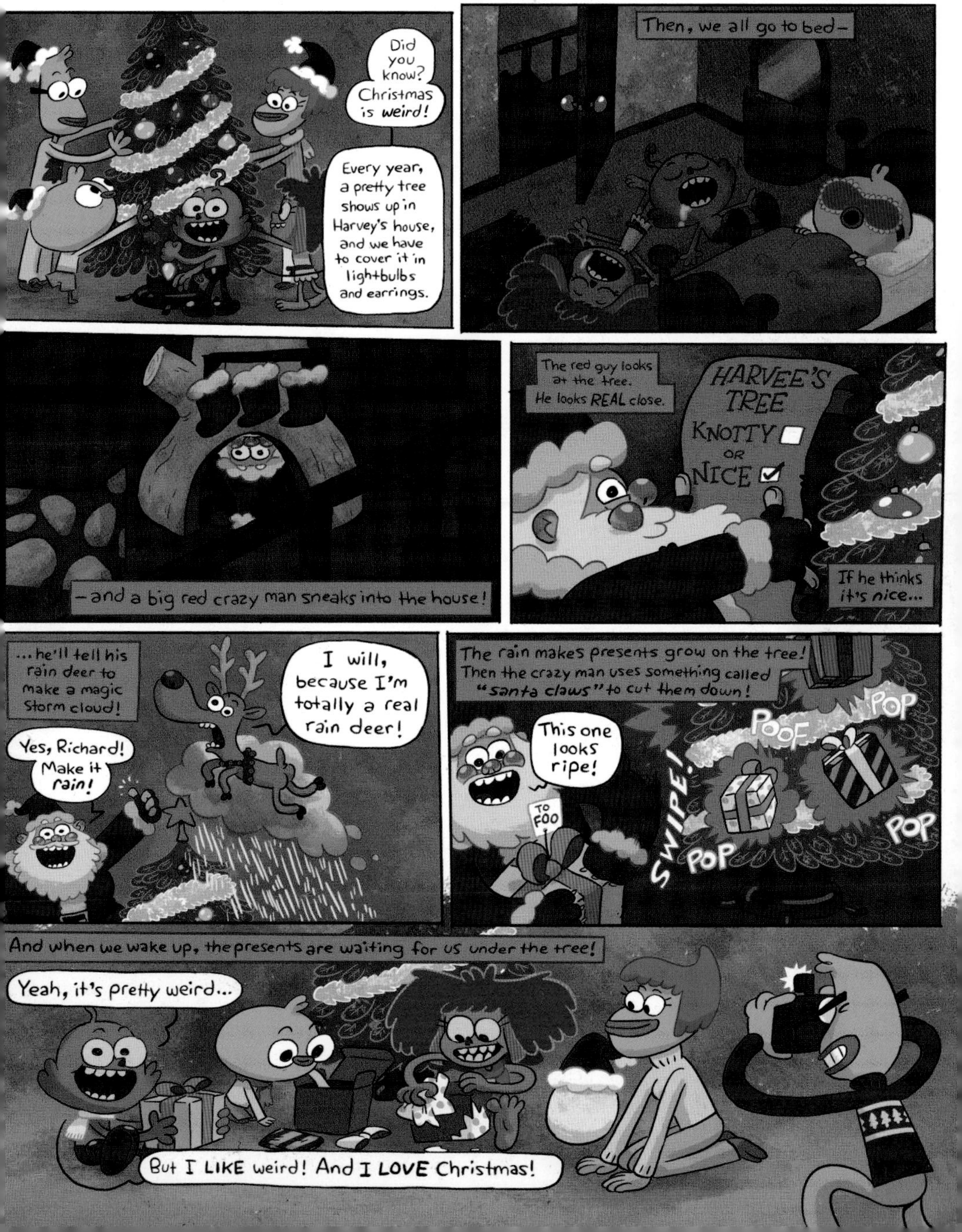

Did you know? Christmas is weird!
Every year, a pretty tree shows up in Harvey's house, and we have to cover it in lightbulbs and earrings.
Then, we all go to bed—
—and a big red crazy man sneaks into the house!
The red guy looks at the tree. He looks REAL close.
HARVEE'S TREE
KNOTTY
OR
NICE
If he thinks it's nice...
...he'll tell his rain deer to make a magic storm cloud!
I will, because I'm totally a real rain deer!
Yes, Richard! Make it rain!
The rain makes presents grow on the tree! Then the crazy man uses something called "santa claws" to cut them down!
This one looks ripe!
TO FOO
POOF
POP
SWIPE!
POP
POP
And when we wake up, the presents are waiting for us under the tree!
Yeah, it's pretty weird...
But I LIKE weird! And I LOVE Christmas!

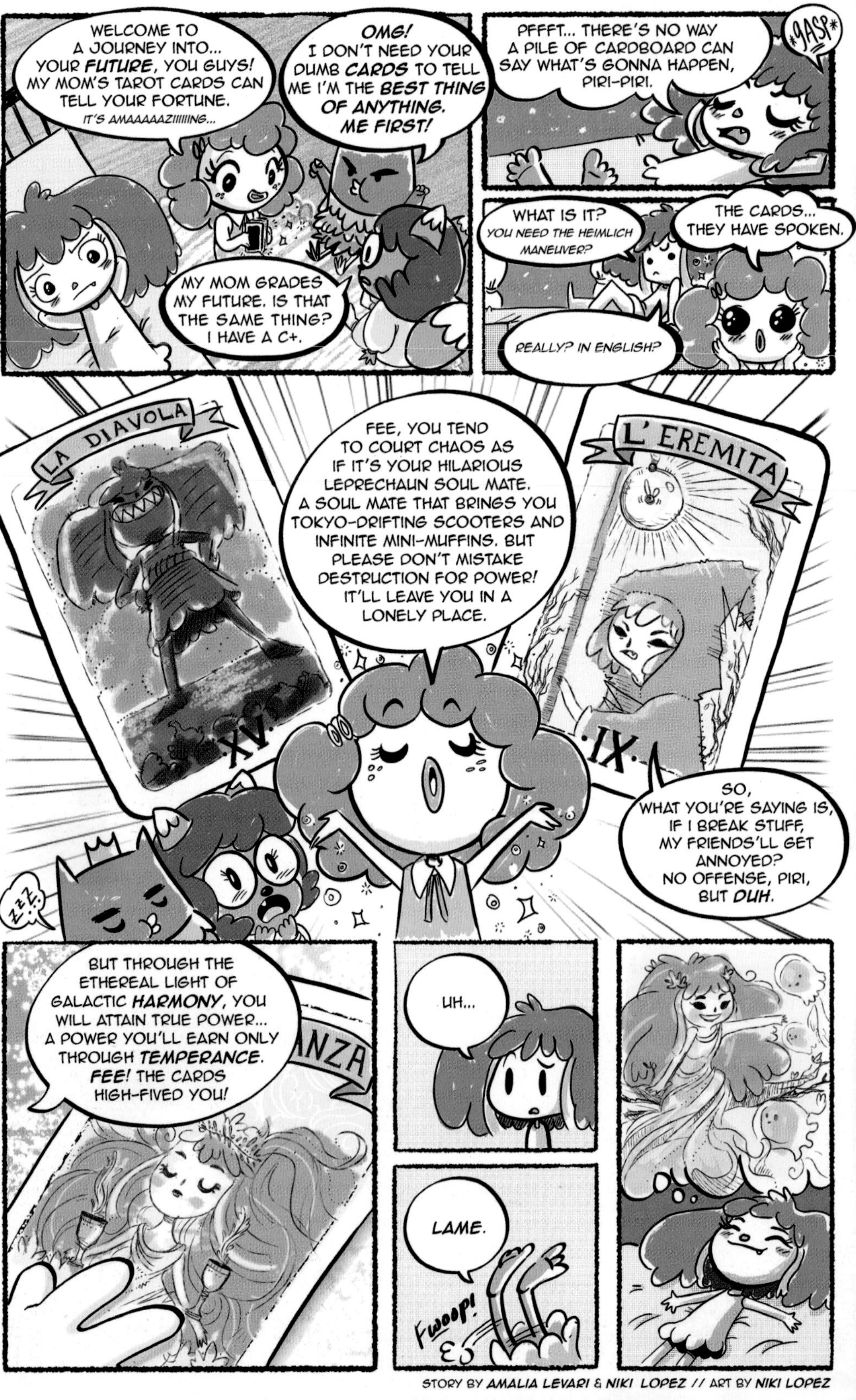
WELCOME TO A JOURNEY INTO... YOUR FUTURE, YOU GUYS! MY MOM'S TAROT CARDS CAN TELL YOUR FORTUNE. IT'S AMAAAAAZIIIIING...
OMG! I DON'T NEED YOUR DUMB CARDS TO TELL ME I'M THE BEST THING OF ANYTHING. ME FIRST!
MY MOM GRADES MY FUTURE. IS THAT THE SAME THING? I HAVE A C+.
PFFFT... THERE'S NO WAY A PILE OF CARDBOARD CAN SAY WHAT'S GONNA HAPPEN, PIRI-PIRI.
GASP
WHAT IS IT? YOU NEED THE HEIMLICH MANEUVER?
THE CARDS... THEY HAVE SPOKEN.
REALLY? IN ENGLISH?
LA DIAVOLA
XV
L' EREMITA
IX
FEE, YOU TEND TO COURT CHAOS AS IF IT'S YOUR HILARIOUS LEPRECHAUN SOUL MATE. A SOUL MATE THAT BRINGS YOU TOKYO-DRIFTING SCOOTERS AND INFINITE MINI-MUFFINS. BUT PLEASE DON'T MISTAKE DESTRUCTION FOR POWER! IT'LL LEAVE YOU IN A LONELY PLACE.
SO, WHAT YOU'RE SAYING IS, IF I BREAK STUFF, MY FRIENDS'LL GET ANNOYED? NO OFFENSE, PIRI, BUT DUH.
ZZZ
BUT THROUGH THE ETHEREAL LIGHT OF GALACTIC HARMONY, YOU WILL ATTAIN TRUE POWER... A POWER YOU'LL EARN ONLY THROUGH TEMPERANCE. FEE! THE CARDS HIGH-FIVED YOU!
ANZA
UH...
LAME.
FWOOP!

STORY BY AMALIA LEVARI & NIKI LOPEZ // ART BY NIKI LOPEZ

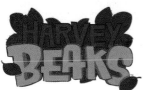

HARVEY BEAKS

PRINCESS'S DIARY

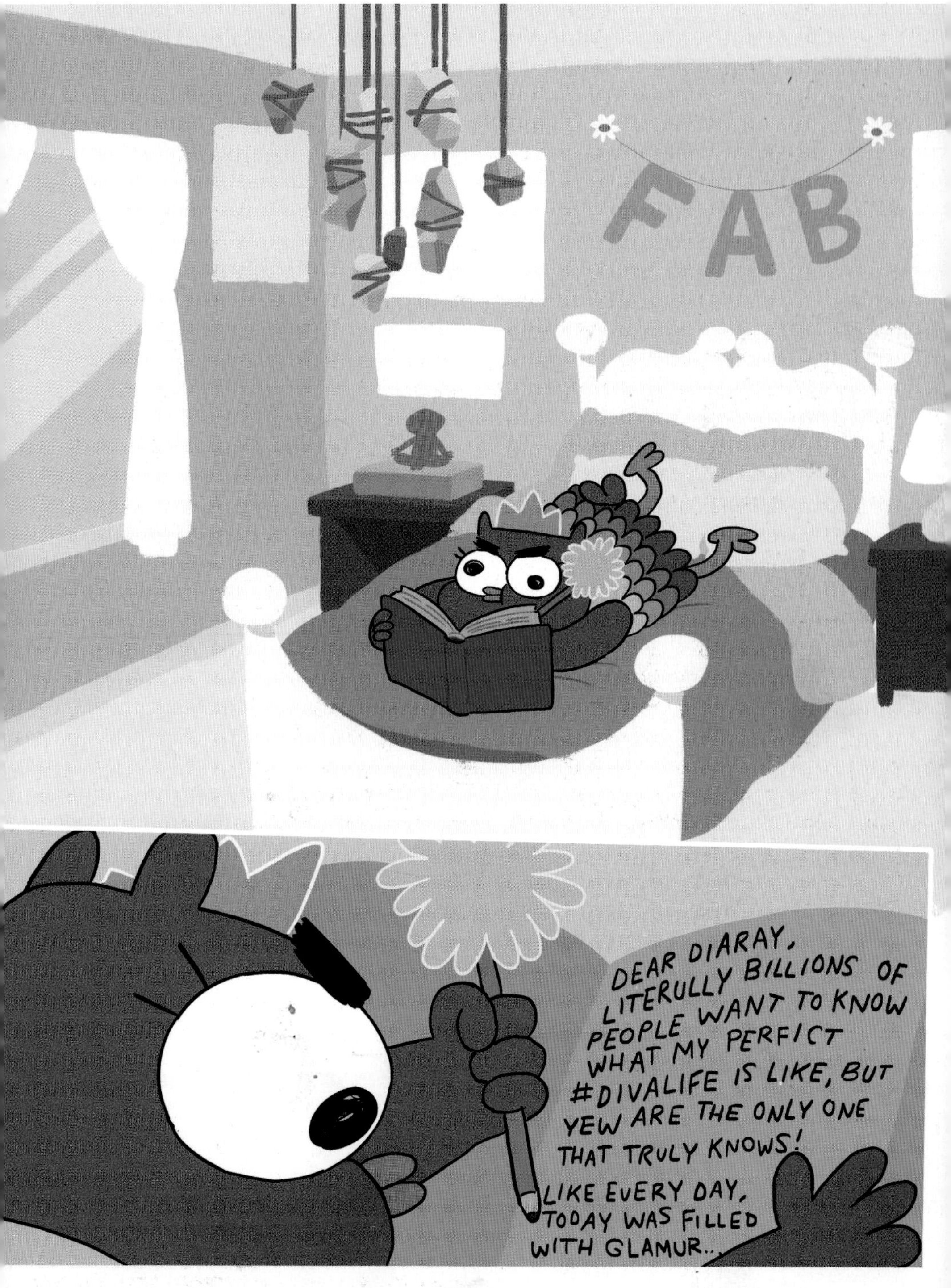
FAB
DEAR DIARAY,
LITERULLY BILLIONS OF PEOPLE WANT TO KNOW WHAT MY PERFICT #DIVALIFE IS LIKE, BUT YEW ARE THE ONLY ONE THAT TRULY KNOWS!
LIKE EVERY DAY, TODAY WAS FILLED WITH GLAMUR..

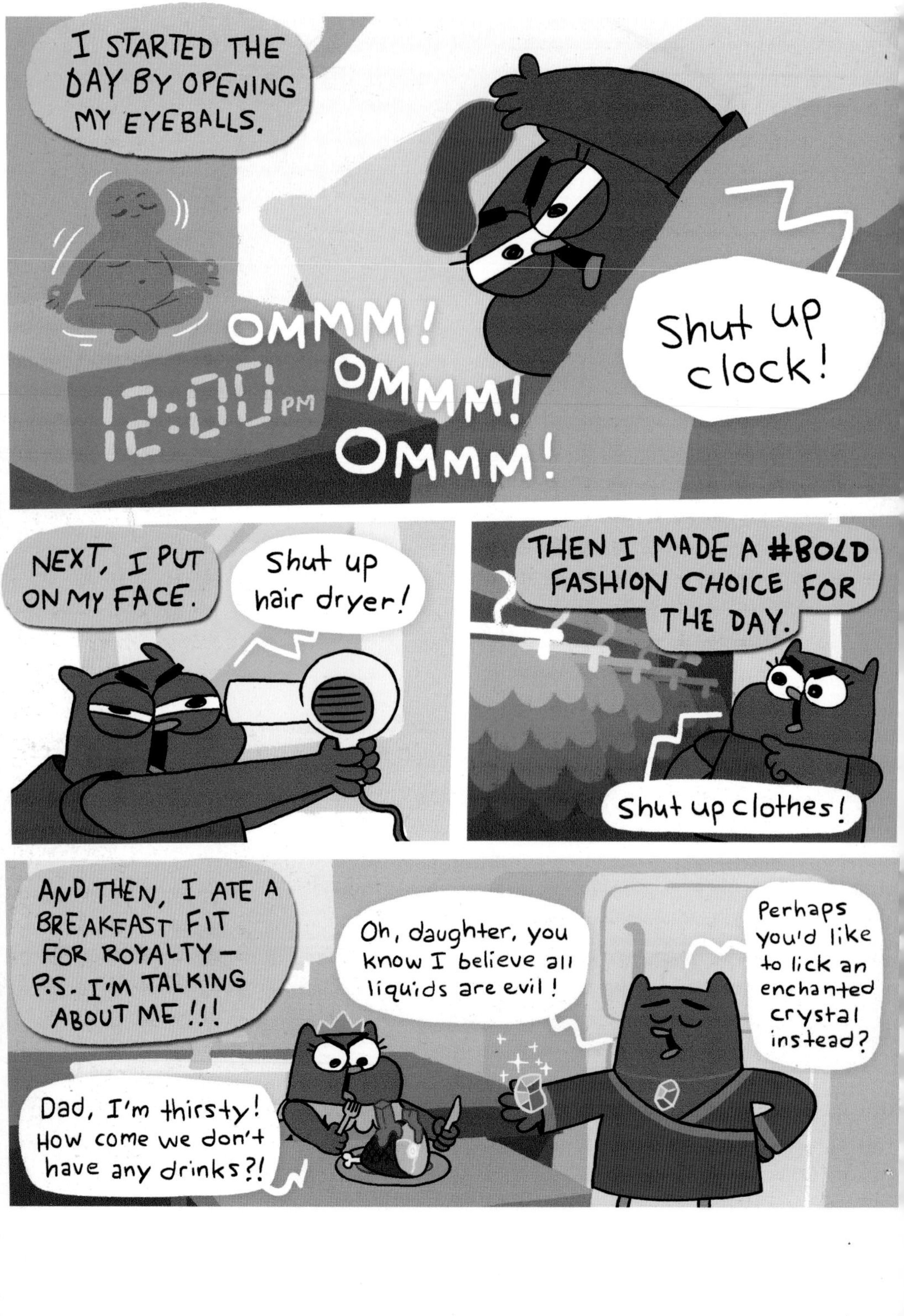
I STARTED THE DAY BY OPENING MY EYEBALLS.
OMMM! OMMM! OMMM!
12:00 PM
Shut up clock!
NEXT, I PUT ON MY FACE.
Shut up hair dryer!
THEN I MADE A #BOLD FASHION CHOICE FOR THE DAY.
Shut up clothes!
AND THEN, I ATE A BREAKFAST FIT FOR ROYALTY — P.S. I'M TALKING ABOUT ME!!!
Dad, I'm thirsty! How come we don't have any drinks?!
Oh, daughter, you know I believe all liquids are evil!
Perhaps you'd like to lick an enchanted crystal instead?

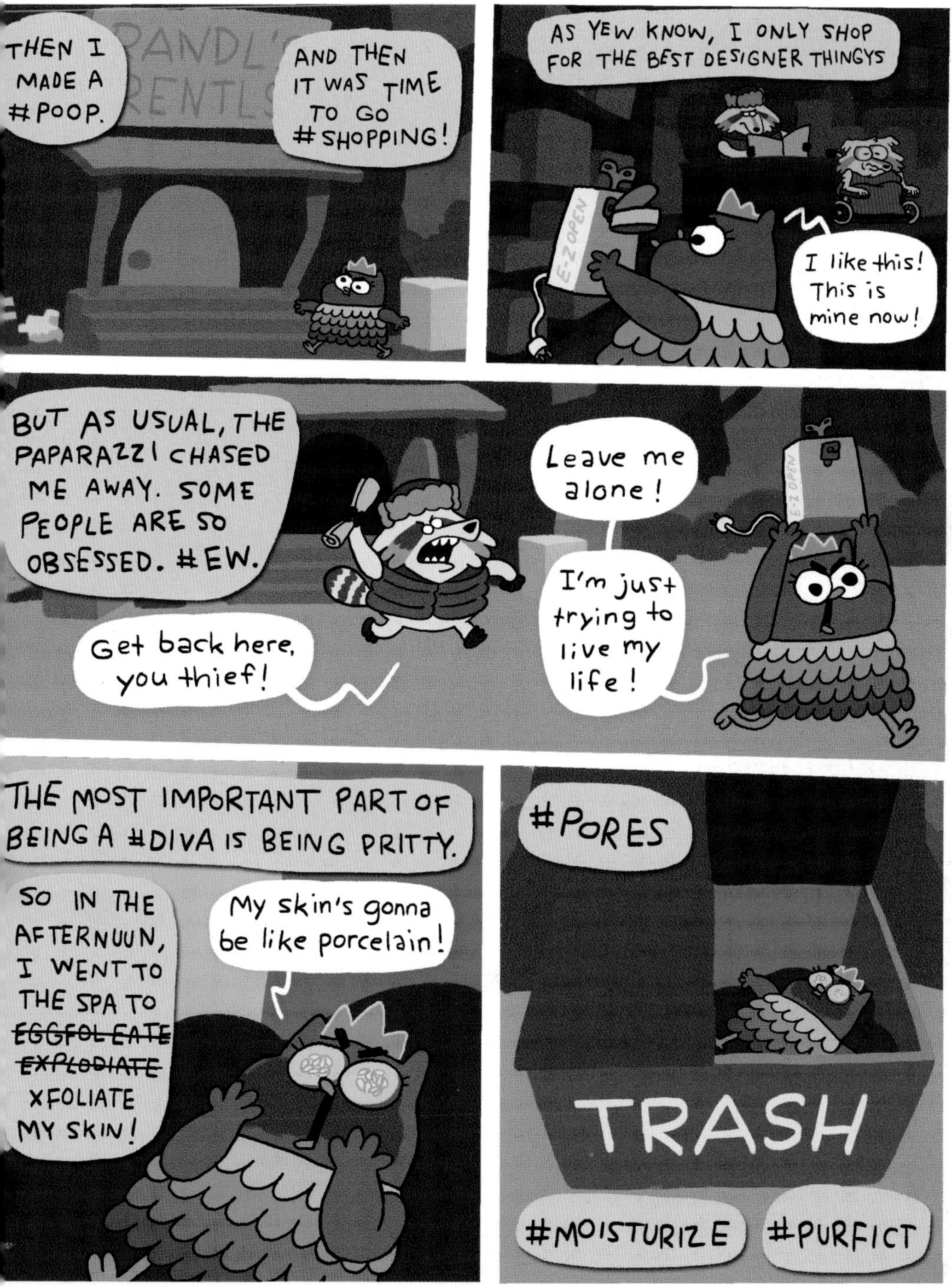
THEN I MADE A #POOP.
AND THEN IT WAS TIME TO GO #SHOPPING!
AS YEW KNOW, I ONLY SHOP FOR THE BEST DESIGNER THINGYS
I like this! This is mine now!
BUT AS USUAL, THE PAPARAZZI CHASED ME AWAY. SOME PEOPLE ARE SO OBSESSED. #EW.
Get back here, you thief!
Leave me alone!
I'm just trying to live my life!
THE MOST IMPORTANT PART OF BEING A #DIVA IS BEING PRITTY.
SO IN THE AFTERNUUN, I WENT TO THE SPA TO ~~EGGFOLEATE~~ ~~EXPLODIATE~~ XFOLIATE MY SKIN!
My skin's gonna be like porcelain!
#PORES
TRASH
#MOISTURIZE
#PURFICT

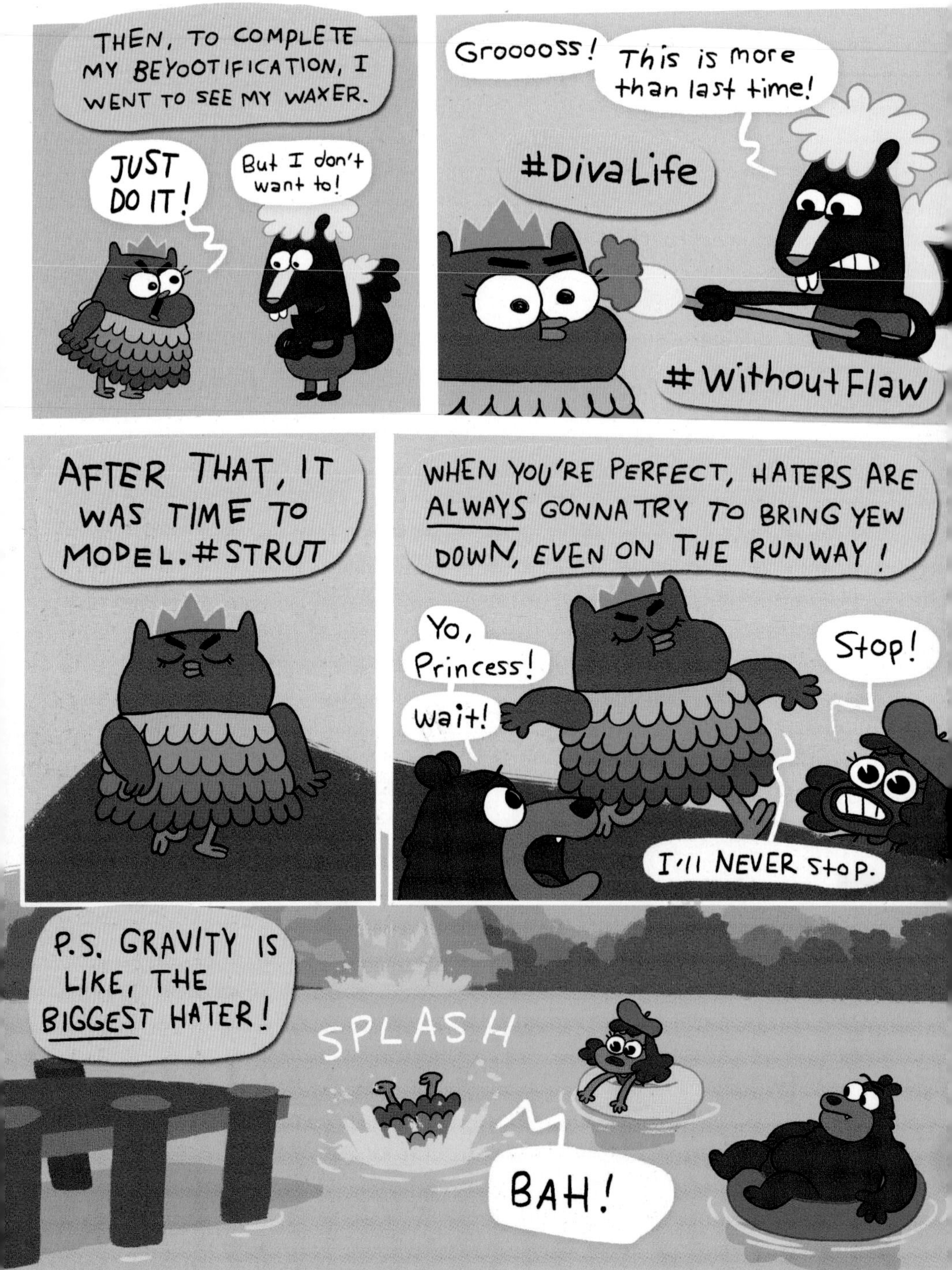
THEN, TO COMPLETE MY BEYOOTIFICATION, I WENT TO SEE MY WAXER.
JUST DO IT!
But I don't want to!
Grooooss!
This is more than last time!
#DivaLife
#WithoutFlaw
AFTER THAT, IT WAS TIME TO MODEL. #STRUT
WHEN YOU'RE PERFECT, HATERS ARE ALWAYS GONNA TRY TO BRING YEW DOWN, EVEN ON THE RUNWAY!
Yo, Princess!
wait!
Stop!
I'll NEVER stop.
P.S. GRAVITY IS LIKE, THE BIGGEST HATER!
SPLASH
BAH!

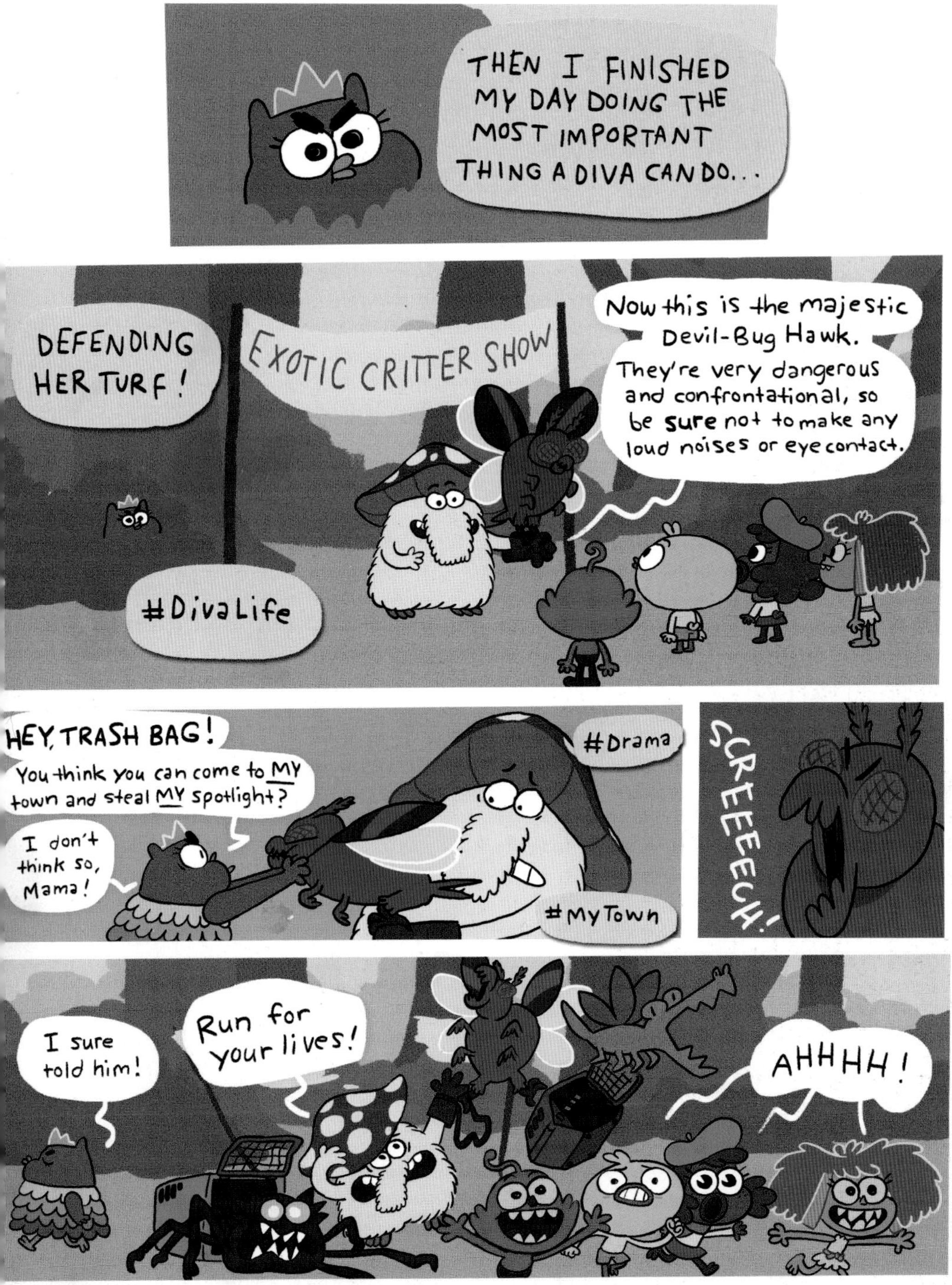
THEN I FINISHED MY DAY DOING THE MOST IMPORTANT THING A DIVA CAN DO...
DEFENDING HER TURF!
EXOTIC CRITTER SHOW
Now this is the majestic Devil-Bug Hawk.
They're very dangerous and confrontational, so be **sure** not to make any loud noises or eye contact.
#DivaLife
HEY, TRASH BAG!
You think you can come to MY town and steal MY spotlight?
I don't think so, Mama!
#Drama
#MyTown
SCREEEEECH!
I sure told him!
Run for your lives!
AHHHH!

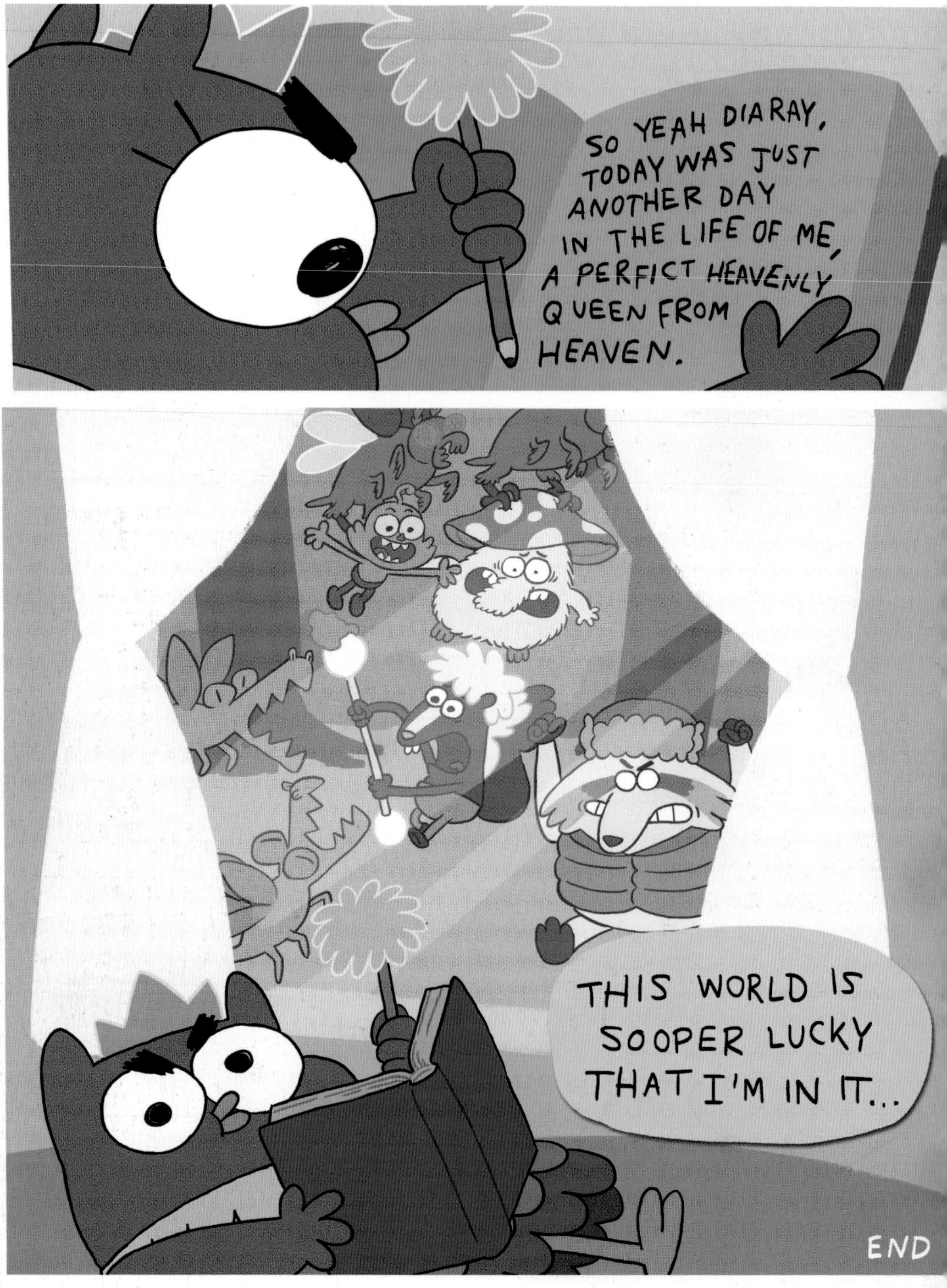
SO YEAH DIARAY, TODAY WAS JUST ANOTHER DAY IN THE LIFE OF ME, A PERFICT HEAVENLY QUEEN FROM HEAVEN.
THIS WORLD IS SOOPER LUCKY THAT I'M IN IT...
END

FOO FACT # 39 – CANDY CANES

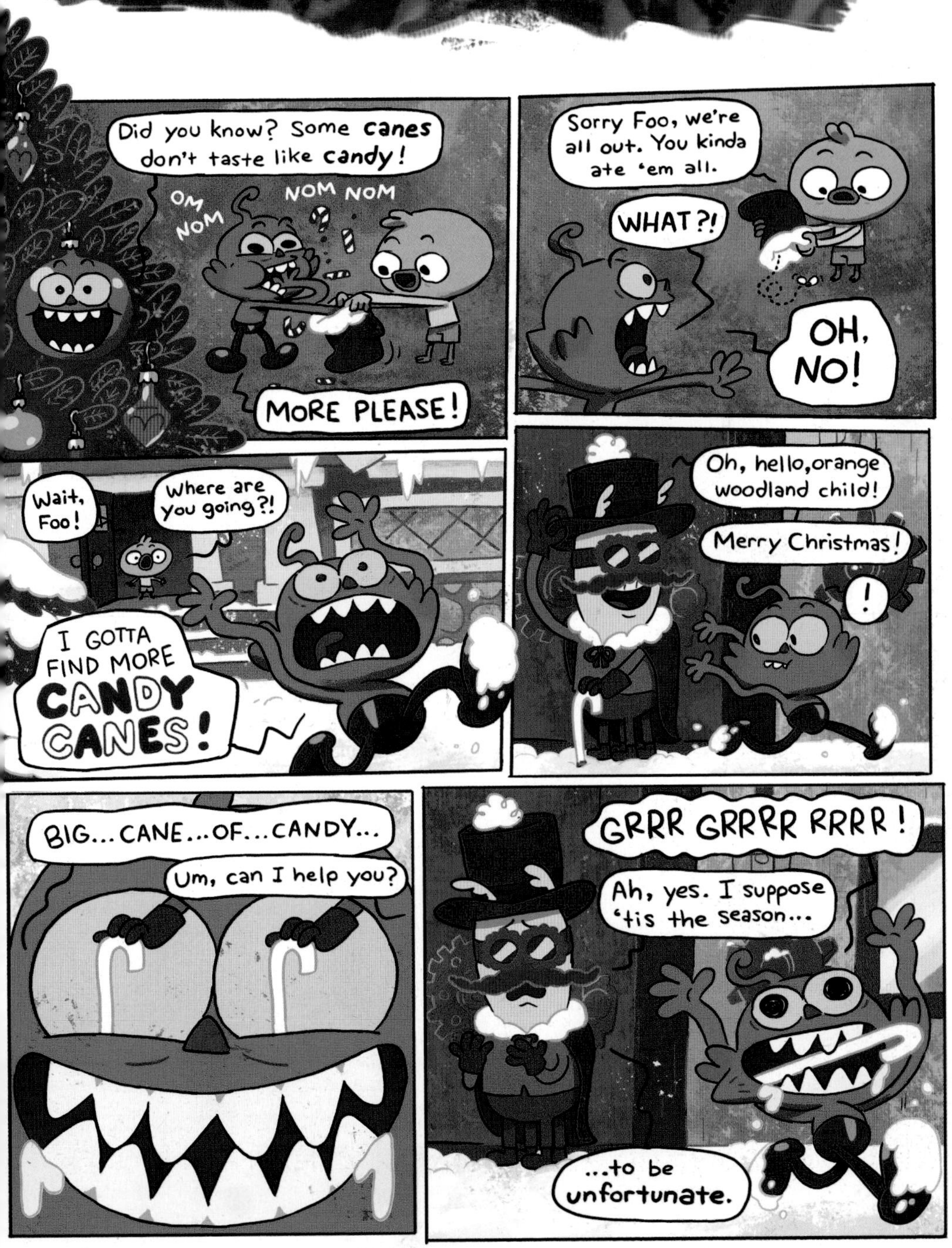
Did you know? Some canes don't taste like candy!
OM NOM
NOM NOM
MORE PLEASE!
Sorry Foo, we're all out. You kinda ate 'em all.
WHAT?!
OH, NO!
Wait, Foo!
Where are you going?!
I GOTTA FIND MORE CANDY CANES!
Oh, hello, orange woodland child!
Merry Christmas!
!
BIG... CANE... OF... CANDY...
Um, can I help you?
GRRR GRRRR RRRR!
Ah, yes. I suppose 'tis the season...
...to be unfortunate.

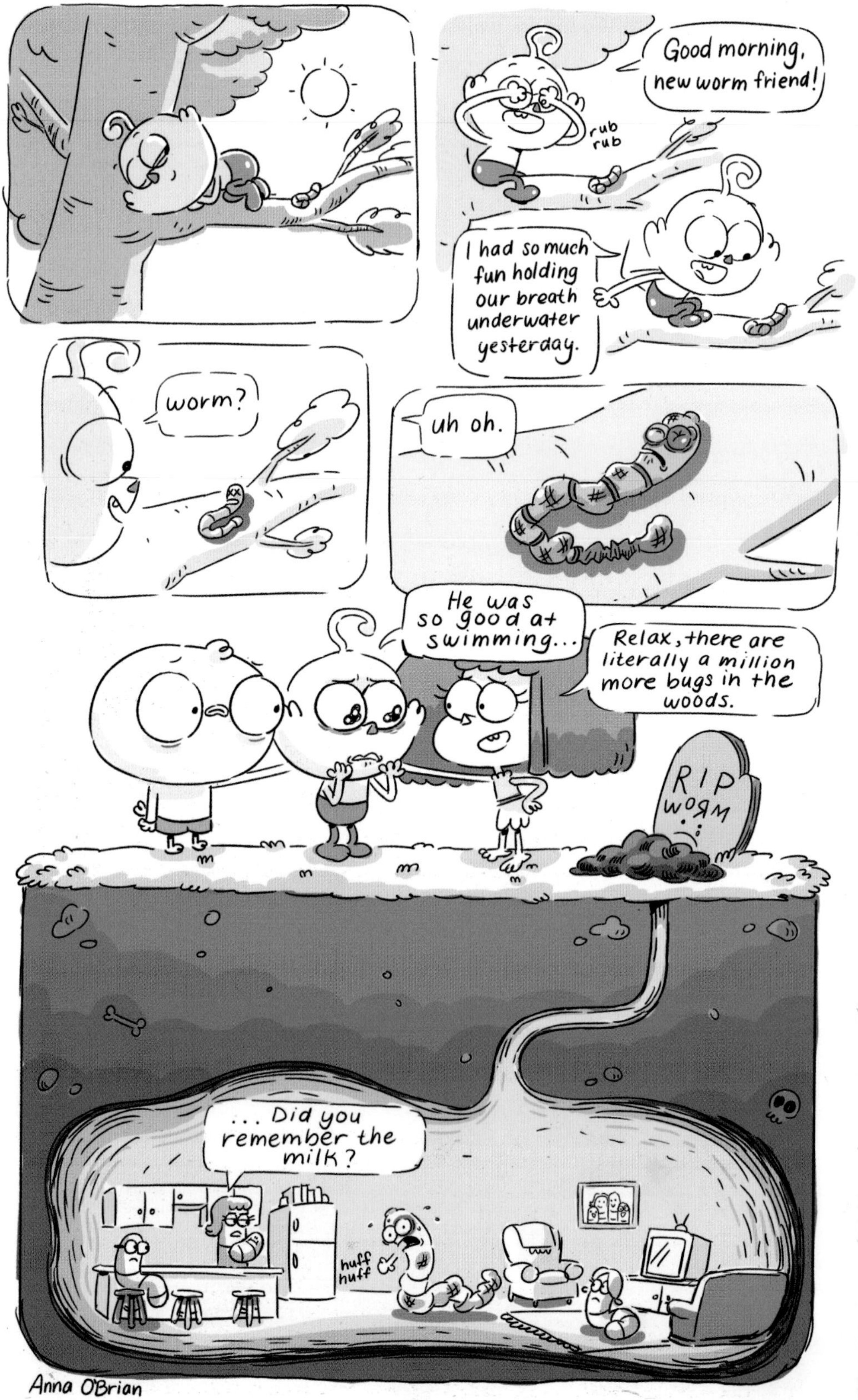
Good morning, new worm friend!
rub rub
I had so much fun holding our breath underwater yesterday.
worm?
uh oh.
He was so good at swimming...
Relax, there are literally a million more bugs in the woods.
RIP WORM
... Did you remember the milk?
huff huff

Anna O'Brian

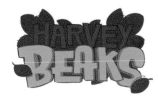

EVIL TWIN

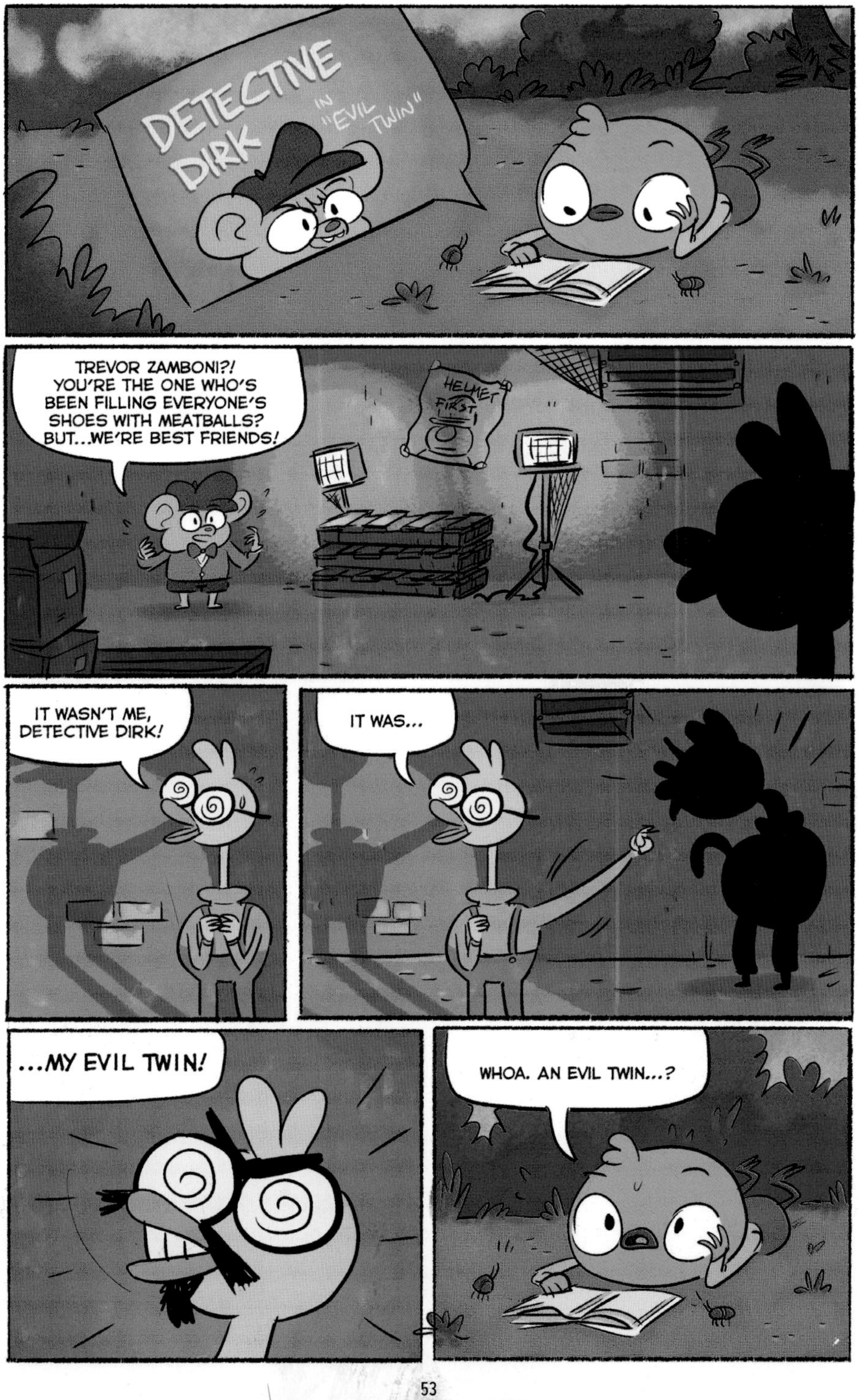
DETECTIVE DIRK
IN "EVIL TWIN"
TREVOR ZAMBONI?! YOU'RE THE ONE WHO'S BEEN FILLING EVERYONE'S SHOES WITH MEATBALLS? BUT...WE'RE BEST FRIENDS!
HELMET FIRST
IT WASN'T ME, DETECTIVE DIRK!
IT WAS...
...MY EVIL TWIN!
WHOA. AN EVIL TWIN...?

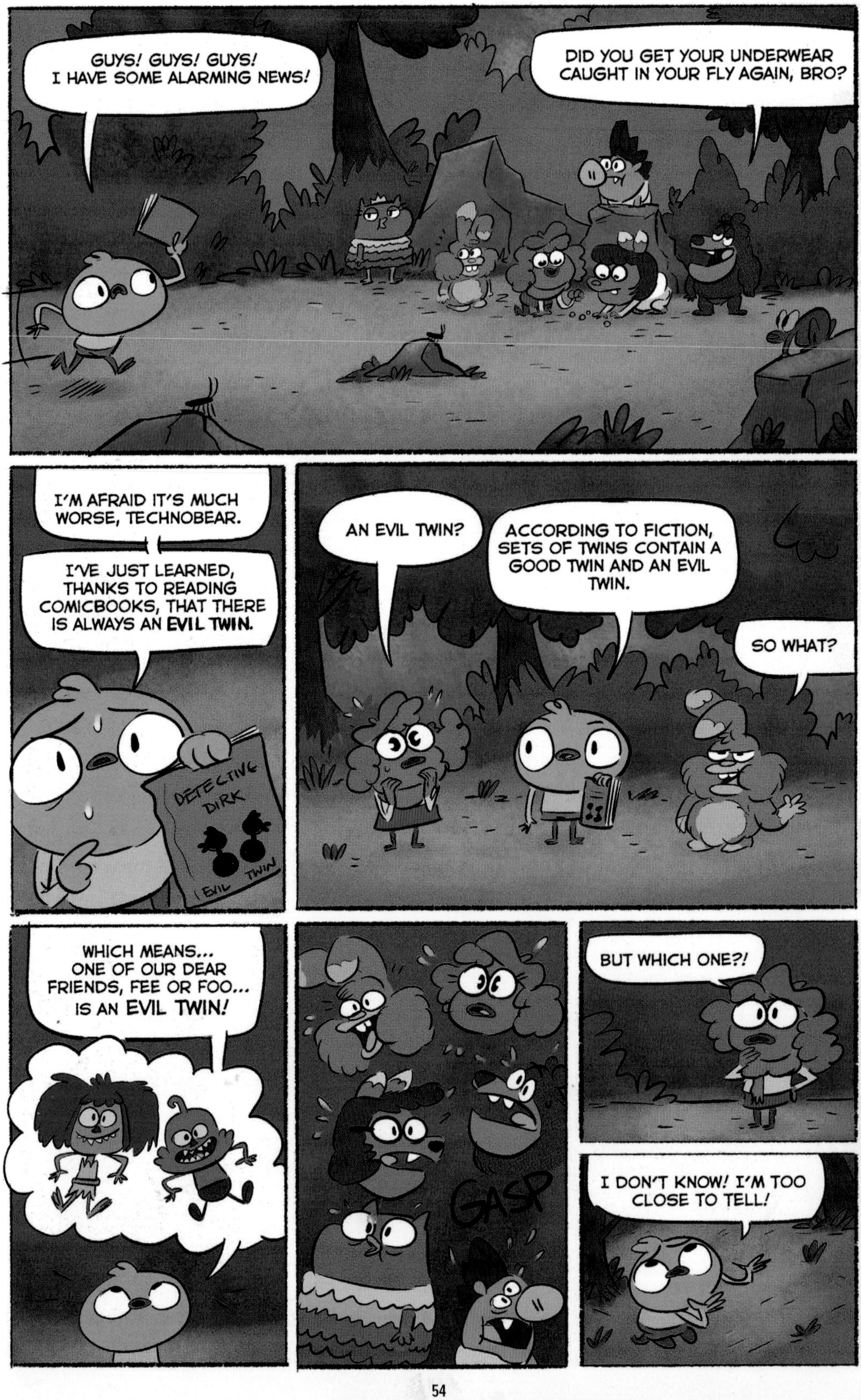
GUYS! GUYS! GUYS! I HAVE SOME ALARMING NEWS!
DID YOU GET YOUR UNDERWEAR CAUGHT IN YOUR FLY AGAIN, BRO?
I'M AFRAID IT'S MUCH WORSE, TECHNOBEAR.
I'VE JUST LEARNED, THANKS TO READING COMICBOOKS, THAT THERE IS ALWAYS AN **EVIL TWIN.**
DETECTIVE DIRK
EVIL TWIN
AN EVIL TWIN?
ACCORDING TO FICTION, SETS OF TWINS CONTAIN A GOOD TWIN AND AN EVIL TWIN.
SO WHAT?
WHICH MEANS... ONE OF OUR DEAR FRIENDS, FEE OR FOO... IS AN **EVIL TWIN!**
GASP
BUT WHICH ONE?!
I DON'T KNOW! I'M TOO CLOSE TO TELL!

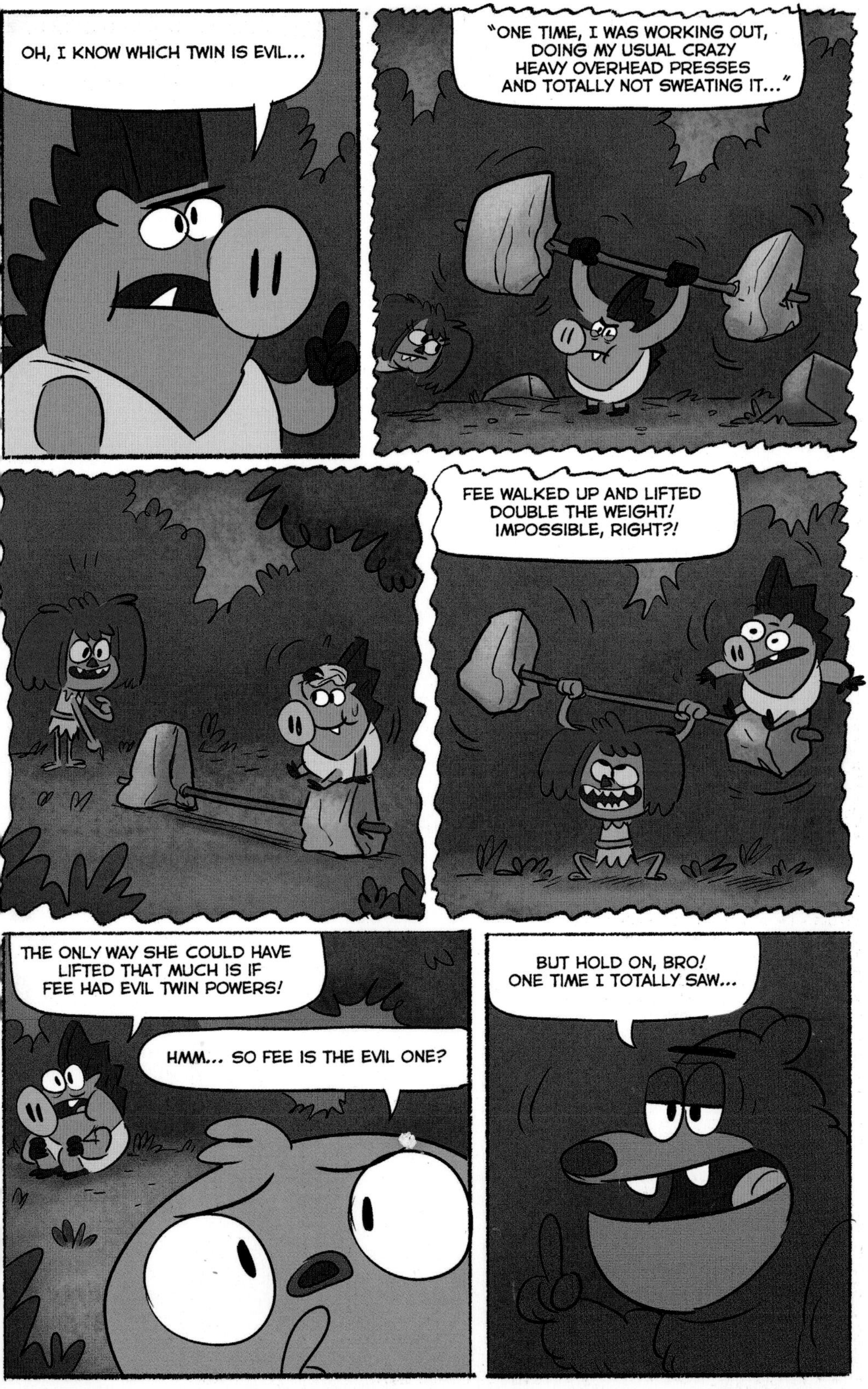
OH, I KNOW WHICH TWIN IS EVIL...
"ONE TIME, I WAS WORKING OUT, DOING MY USUAL CRAZY HEAVY OVERHEAD PRESSES AND TOTALLY NOT SWEATING IT..."
FEE WALKED UP AND LIFTED DOUBLE THE WEIGHT! IMPOSSIBLE, RIGHT?!
THE ONLY WAY SHE COULD HAVE LIFTED THAT MUCH IS IF FEE HAD EVIL TWIN POWERS!
HMM... SO FEE IS THE EVIL ONE?
BUT HOLD ON, BRO! ONE TIME I TOTALLY SAW...

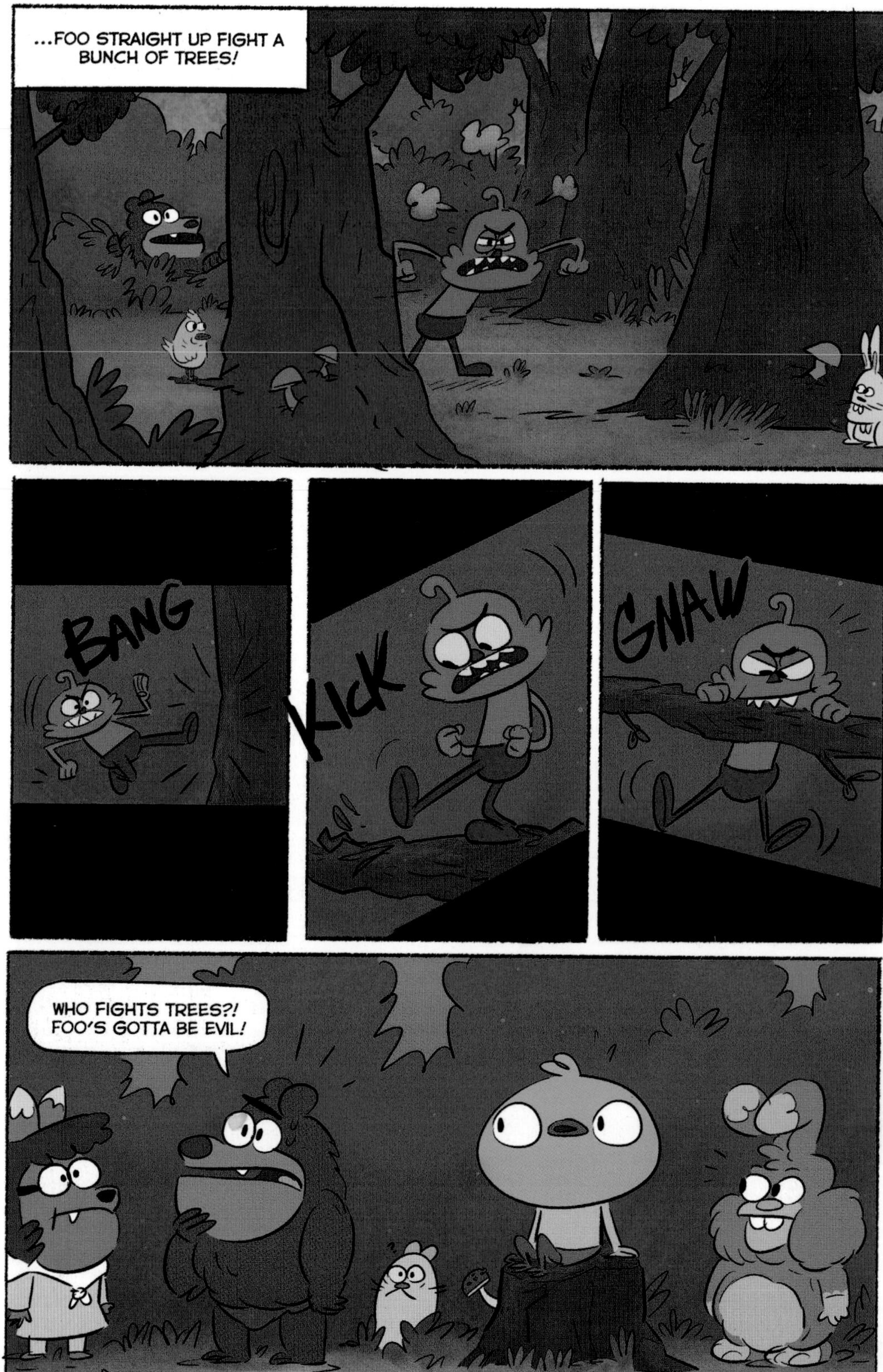
...FOO STRAIGHT UP FIGHT A BUNCH OF TREES!
BANG
KICK
GNAW
WHO FIGHTS TREES?! FOO'S GOTTA BE EVIL!

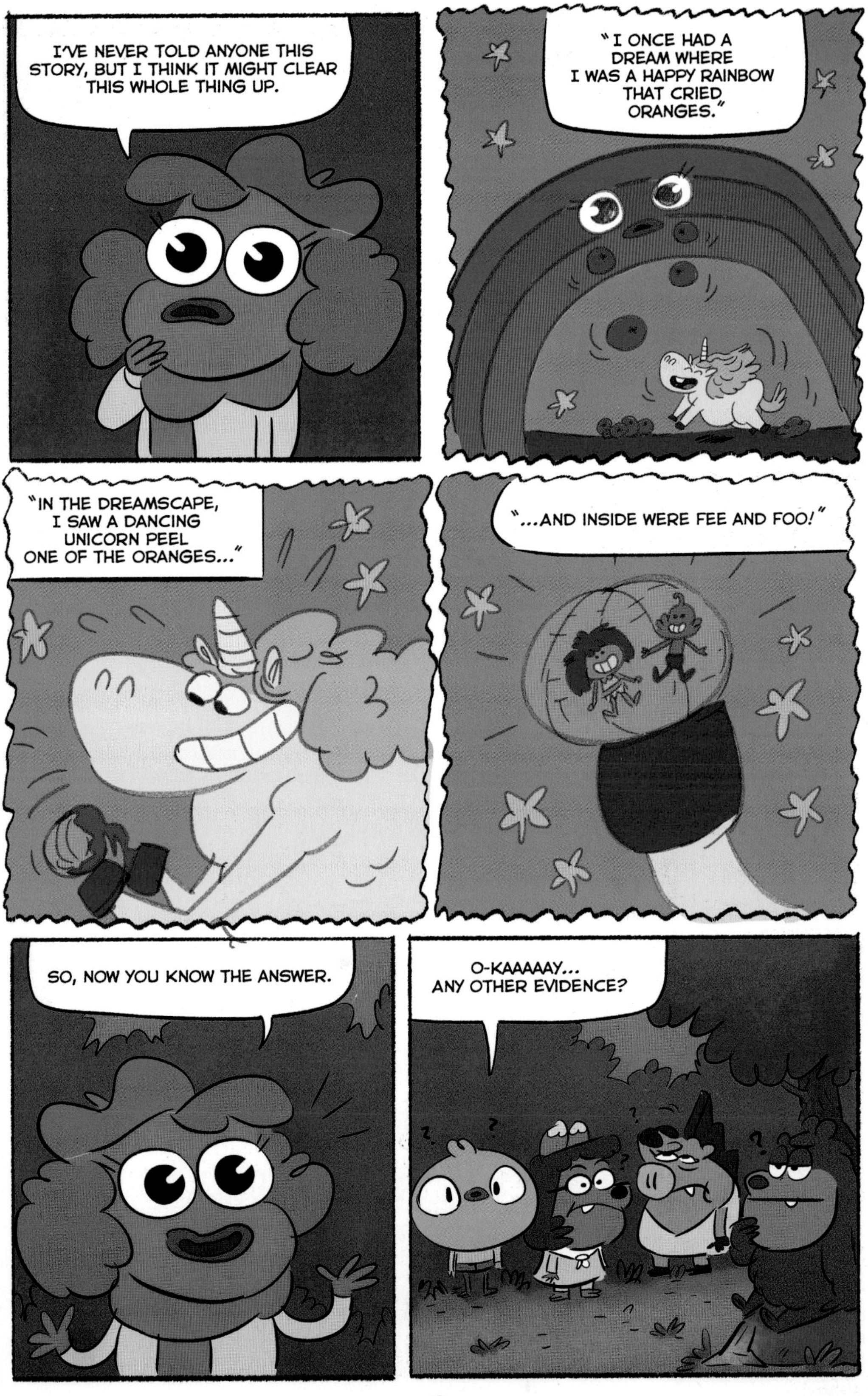
I'VE NEVER TOLD ANYONE THIS STORY, BUT I THINK IT MIGHT CLEAR THIS WHOLE THING UP.
"I ONCE HAD A DREAM WHERE I WAS A HAPPY RAINBOW THAT CRIED ORANGES."
"IN THE DREAMSCAPE, I SAW A DANCING UNICORN PEEL ONE OF THE ORANGES..."
"...AND INSIDE WERE FEE AND FOO!"
SO, NOW YOU KNOW THE ANSWER.
O-KAAAAAY... ANY OTHER EVIDENCE?

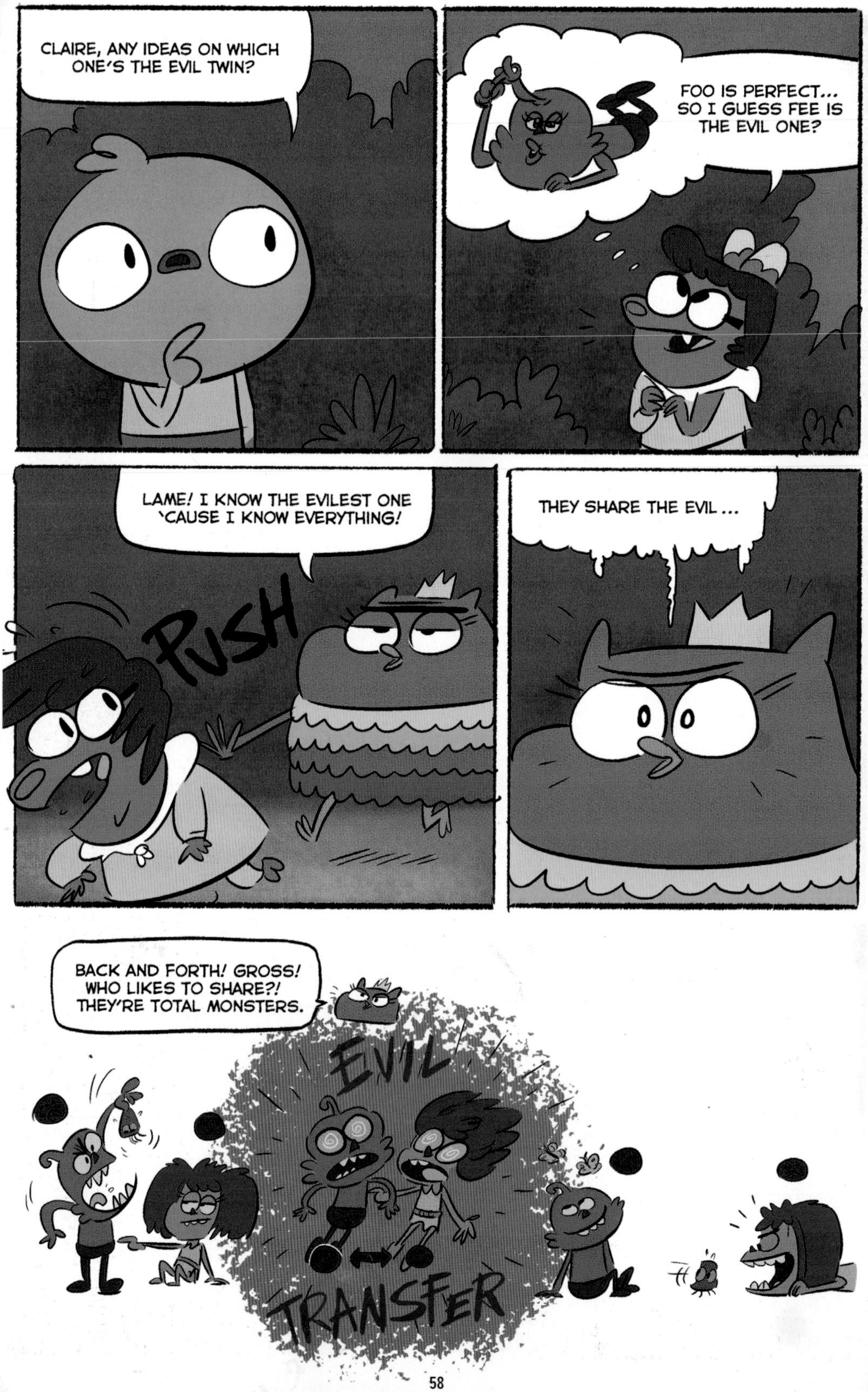
CLAIRE, ANY IDEAS ON WHICH ONE'S THE EVIL TWIN?
FOO IS PERFECT... SO I GUESS FEE IS THE EVIL ONE?
LAME! I KNOW THE EVILEST ONE 'CAUSE I KNOW EVERYTHING!
PUSH
THEY SHARE THE EVIL ...
BACK AND FORTH! GROSS! WHO LIKES TO SHARE?! THEY'RE TOTAL MONSTERS.
EVIL
TRANSFER

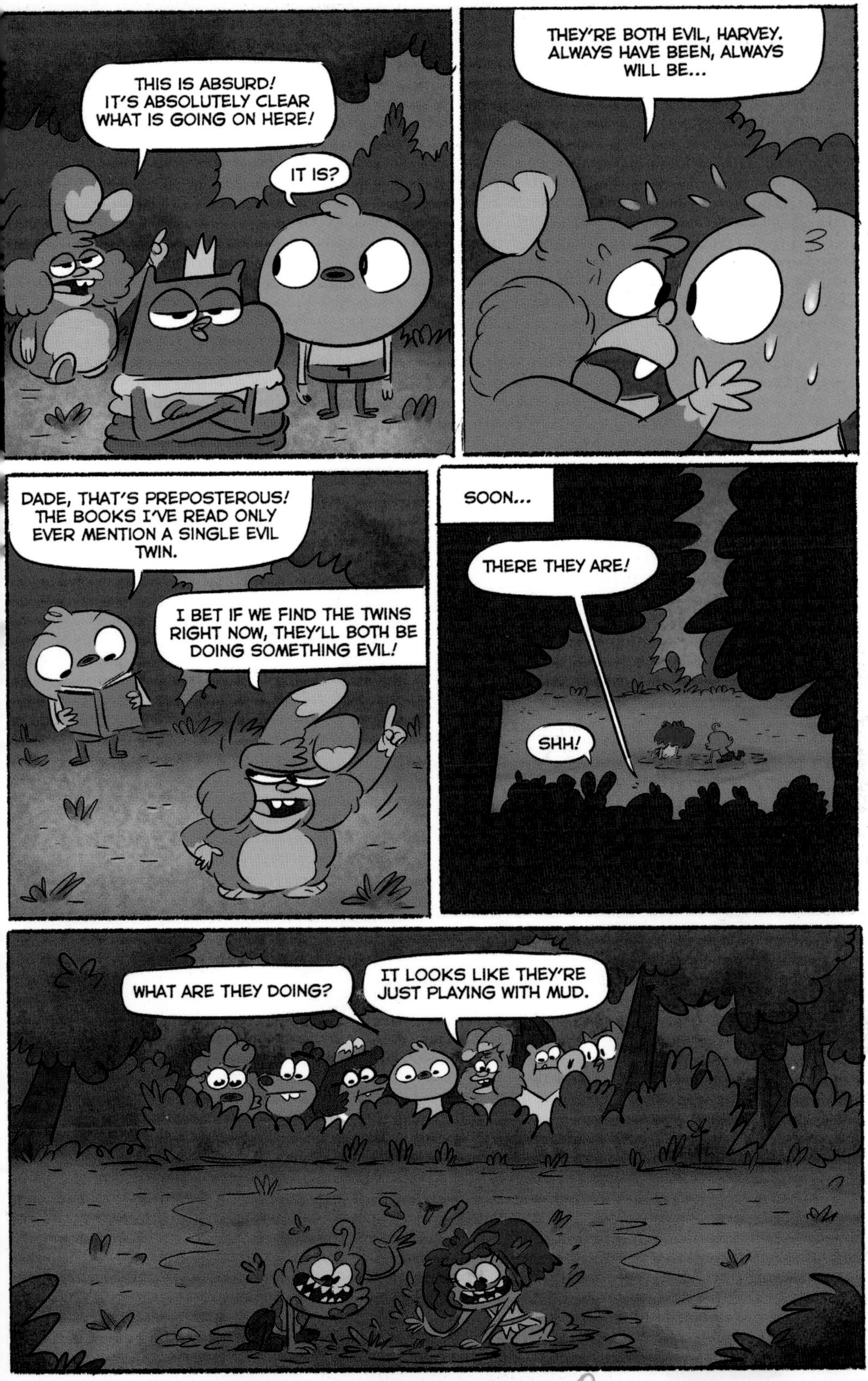
THIS IS ABSURD! IT'S ABSOLUTELY CLEAR WHAT IS GOING ON HERE!
IT IS?
THEY'RE BOTH EVIL, HARVEY. ALWAYS HAVE BEEN, ALWAYS WILL BE...
DADE, THAT'S PREPOSTEROUS! THE BOOKS I'VE READ ONLY EVER MENTION A SINGLE EVIL TWIN.
I BET IF WE FIND THE TWINS RIGHT NOW, THEY'LL BOTH BE DOING SOMETHING EVIL!
SOON...
THERE THEY ARE!
SHH!
WHAT ARE THEY DOING?
IT LOOKS LIKE THEY'RE JUST PLAYING WITH MUD.

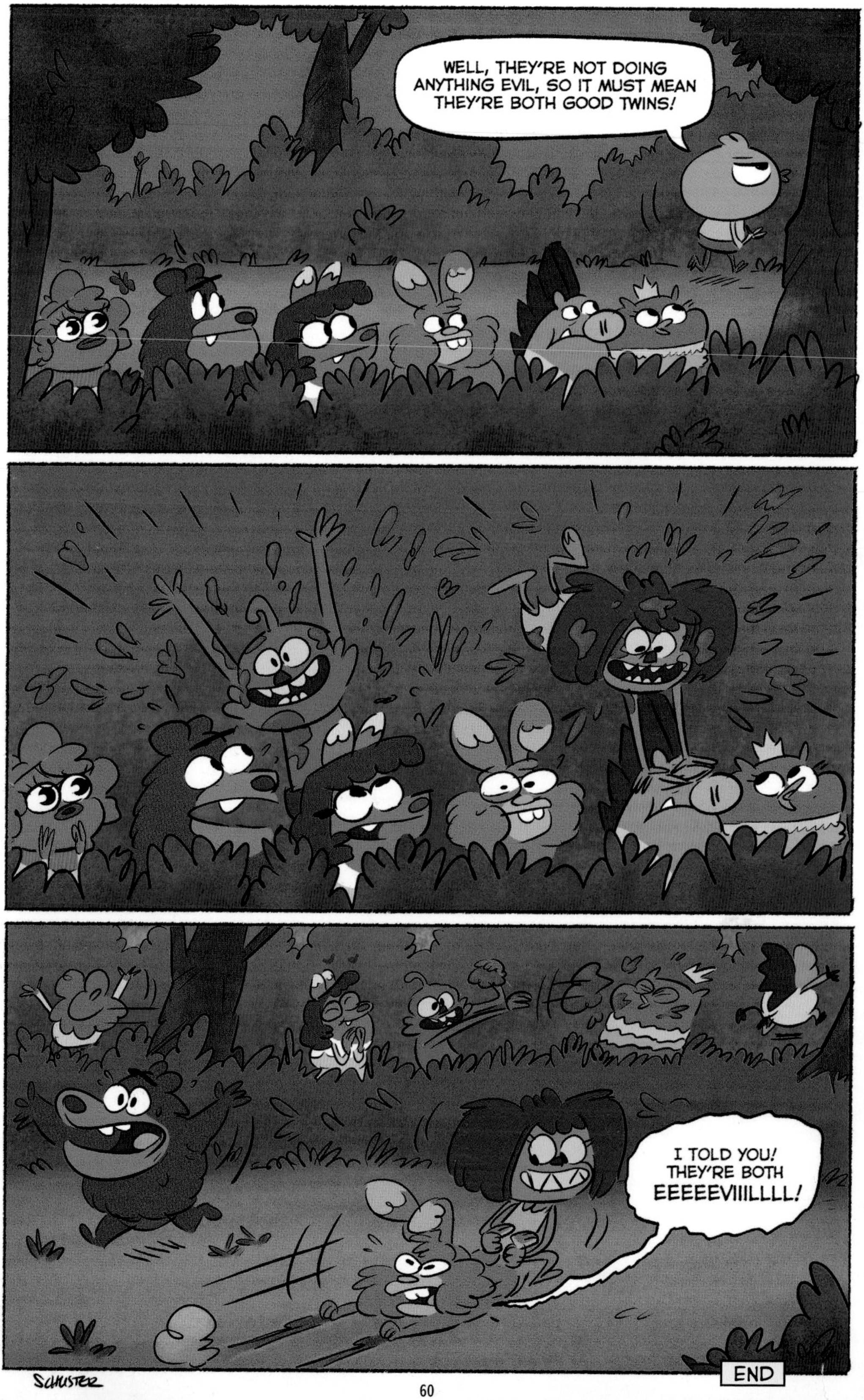
WELL, THEY'RE NOT DOING ANYTHING EVIL, SO IT MUST MEAN THEY'RE BOTH GOOD TWINS!
I TOLD YOU! THEY'RE BOTH EEEEEVIIILLLL!
END
SCHUSTER

WATCH OUT FOR PAPERCUTZ

nickelodeon
PANDEMONIUM!
A COLLECTION OF YOUR FAVORITE TV COMICS

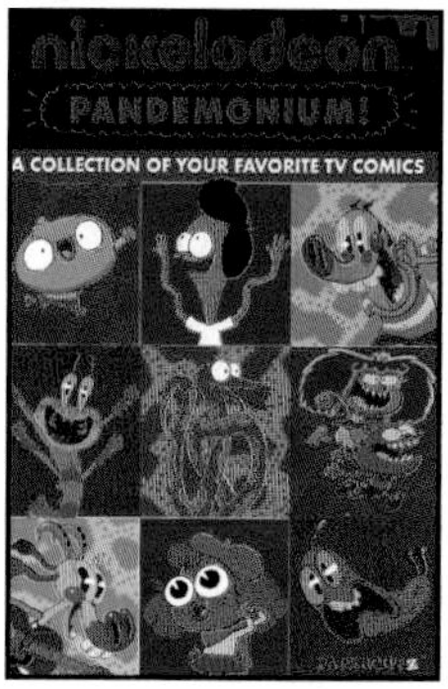

Welcome to the super-sized (at no extra cost to you!) second HARVEY BEAKS graphic novel from Papercutz—those playful people dedicated to publishing great graphic novels for all ages. I'm Jim Salicrup, the risk-averse Editor-in-Chief, and I'm here to take you behind-the-scenes at Papercutz...

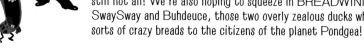

The Big News is that Harvey Beaks will be returning in an all-new graphic novel series entitled NICKELODEON PANDEMONIUM, but that's not all! Also featured in this exciting new series will be Sanjay and Craig—the world's most famous boy (Sanjay Patel) and his talking snake (Craig). But that's still not all! NICKELODEON PANDEMONIUM will also feature Pig, Goat, Banana, Cricket—those prank-loving creatures that we all know and love! And believe it or not, that's still not all! We're also hoping to squeeze in BREADWINNERS—SwaySway and Buhdeuce, those two overly zealous ducks who deliver all sorts of crazy breads to the citizens of the planet Pondgea!

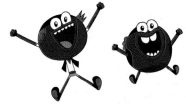

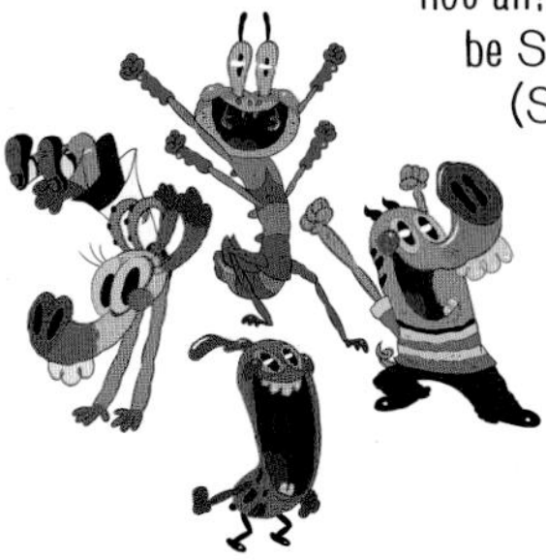

Certainly an announcement this big, this utterly awesome is going to get a tremendous amount of attention, so we suggest that you make sure to let your favorite bookseller know that you want to reserve a copy of NICKELODEON PANDEMONIUM #1, otherwise it may sell out. And then what will you do while you're waiting for it to go back to press? Well, you could order an e-book edition—they never go out of print. Of course, you can keep picking up every issue of NICKELODEON MAGAZINE—but we suspect you're already doing that. After all, it is the best-selling magazine featuring comics of the following Nickelodeon superstars: Sanjay and Craig, Breadwinners, Pig Goat Banana Cricket, and Harvey Beaks! And that's a Foo fact!

One of the coolest things about the NICKELODEON PANDEMONIUM graphic novel series--aside from all the obvious stuff such as presenting great comics created by the best writers and cartoonists in the world today, starring the best and funniest characters, from slime-time TV—is that it'll almost be like watching Nickelodeon on paper, with all-new episodes of your favorite characters! That's just as good as it gets, right?

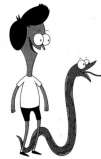

My only concern regarding NICKELODEON PANDEMONIUM is that I hope all that "pandemonium" isn't too much for our good friend Harvey Beaks. He's such a timid soul, after all. But as long as he has Fee and Foo to look out for him, I'm sure he'll be okay! But be sure you join us for the premiere edition of NICKELODEON PANDEMONIUM—because it won't be any fun without YOU!

Thanks,

Jim

STAY IN TOUCH!

EMAIL:	salicrup@papercutz.com
WEB:	papercutz.com
TWITTER:	@papercutzgn
FACEBOOK:	PAPERCUTZGRAPHICNOVELS
FANMAIL:	Papercutz, 160 Broadway, Suite 700, East Wing, New York, NY 10038

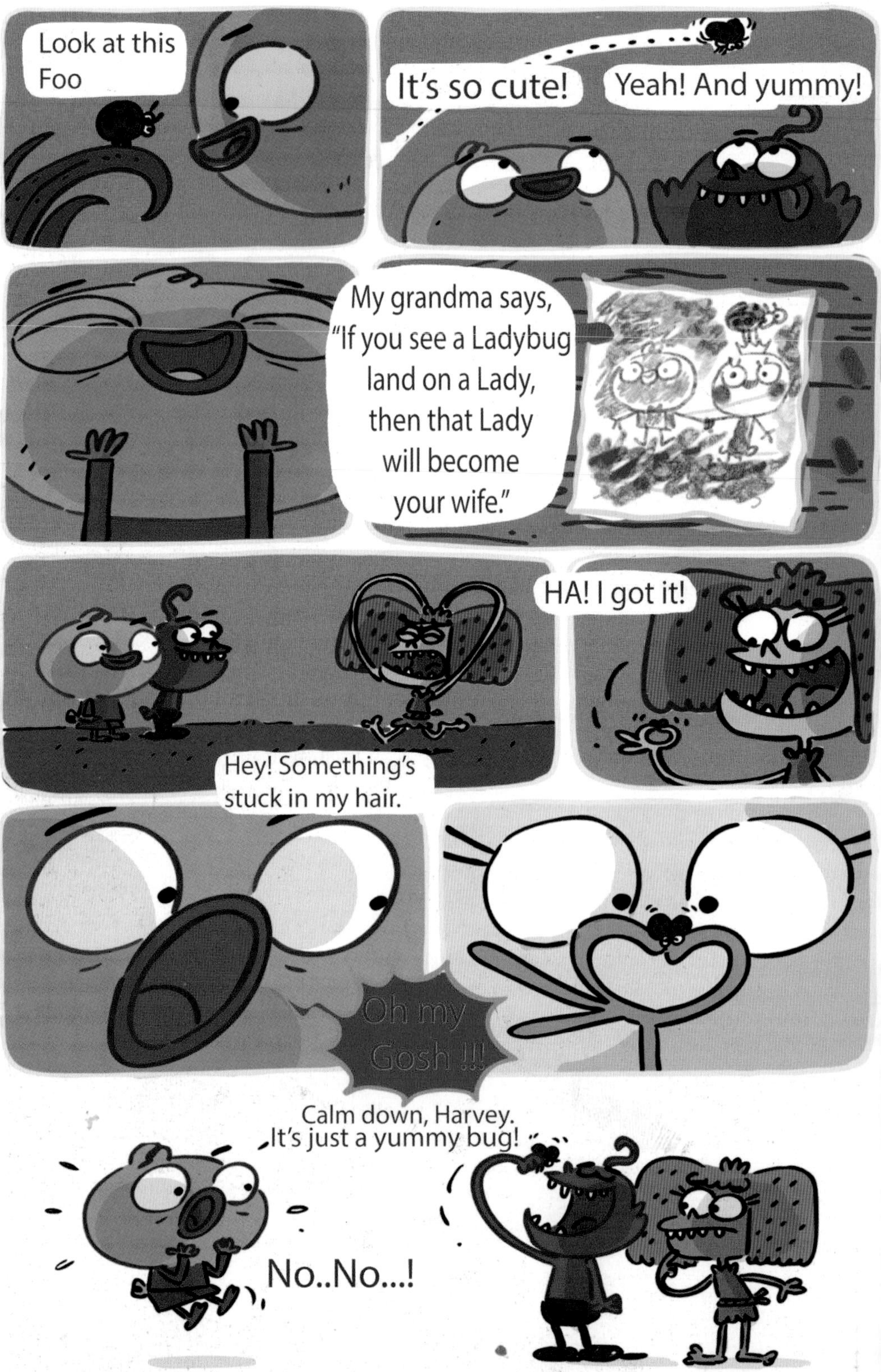
Look at this Foo
It's so cute!
Yeah! And yummy!
My grandma says, "If you see a Ladybug land on a Lady, then that Lady will become your wife."
HA! I got it!
Hey! Something's stuck in my hair.
Oh my Gosh !!!
Calm down, Harvey. It's just a yummy bug!
No..No...!

Special Preview of Pig Goat Banana Cricket "The Bride of Burgerstein" Part One

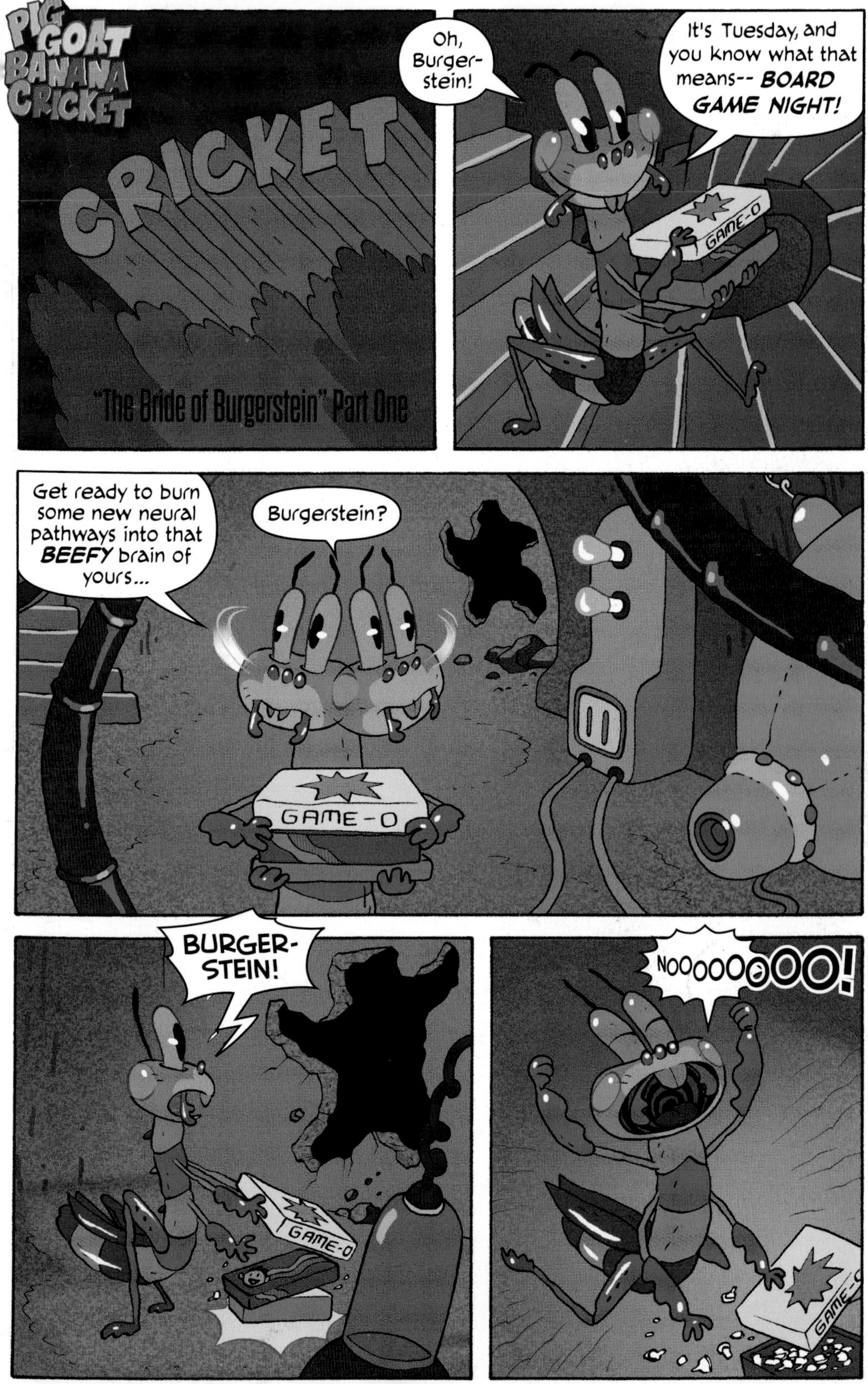
PIG GOAT BANANA CRICKET
CRICKET
"The Bride of Burgerstein" Part One
Oh, Burger-stein!
It's Tuesday, and you know what that means-- BOARD GAME NIGHT!
GAME-O
Get ready to burn some new neural pathways into that BEEFY brain of yours...
Burgerstein?
GAME-O
BURGER-STEIN!
GAME-O
NOOOOOOOOO!
GAME-O

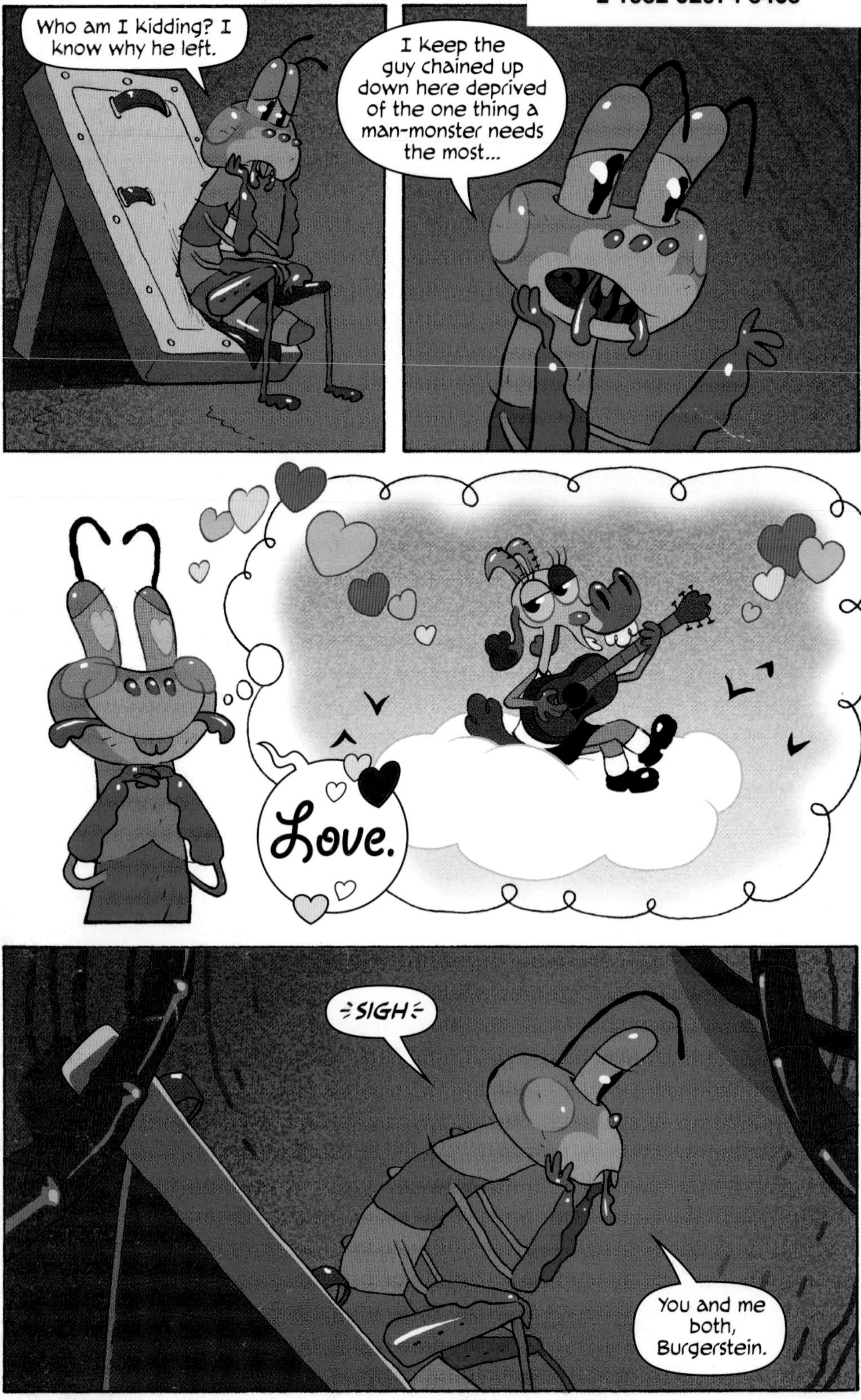
Who am I kidding? I know why he left.
I keep the guy chained up down here deprived of the one thing a man-monster needs the most...
Love.
SIGH
You and me both, Burgerstein.